THE STUFFED CAT AND THE CORPSE WITH NO SHOES

A NOVEL

by
Julia Shaw
Billie Sherman
Will White

Cover design by Peter M. White
Printed by KDP Press

Authors' Note

A Collaborative Novel

Writing fiction with other authors is not new. But in the case of *The Stuffed Cat and the Corpse with No Shoes*, the collaborators' average age is over 90. Two of the authors are poets, and one is a retired advertising copywriter, all friends and fellow residents in a retirement community.

The project, which started as a game, took two years of diplomacy, compromise and good humor to complete. Each author selected individual chapters to write, revising them after review and comments by co-authors. Authors also "adopted" various characters, profiling them and monitoring their depiction by fellow authors.

The plot was not predetermined at the beginning but evolved with weekly proposals and discussion. The end result is a carefully interwoven tapestry written from three perspectives, nourished by a combination of almost three centuries of living and creativity.

1

It was just lying there. A cat. Laid out like a human at a funeral. On its back, front paws crossed over its chest, with a wet newspaper carefully arranged over its lower body, like a blanket in a coffin. There were other "arrangements" too — mainly a loving circle of dying flowers all around the body.

Bernie had been jogging on this early November morning. It was his daily torture. His body was not built for jogging, but Violet kept bugging him about how jogging was good for his cardiovascular health. She even got him to buy an expensive pair of running shoes (which decimated his small savings account.) Okay for her. She never came to the Park, claiming that she got her jogging in on the way to work on the South Side. She was an aide to an environmental activist. Lots of running around, Bernie had to admit. Plastering posters on telephone poles, marching in parades. Didn't pay diddly-shit, but Bernie had long since given up criticizing. It only made Violet defensive; she said it was her moral obligation (even though it didn't do much for the grocery bill). They'd lived together for two years, and Bernie loved her dearly.

Maybe that's why he did this miserable running. Every day. Early in the morning, before a shower and breakfast, because he was the sort who liked to get negative things out of the way as soon as possible.

At least the time and place were not deterrents – at this hour in the morning, hardly anybody else was on the path, and the circuit in the park was easy, a loop maybe a little over a mile around a small pond. Bernie figured that a couple of laps were plenty to serve the great god Exercise.

But the cat threw him off stride, so to speak. He'd seen all sorts of small animals in the park – squirrels, rats, turtles, birds – but very few cats, even strays. What the hell was this feline corpse doing here? Did some distraught neighbor feel compelled to give a pet this elaborate last rite? Was it an eerie joke?

And why the park? Didn't the owner have a back yard? (Or maybe not. There were a lot of apartment dwellers around here.) Bernie looked around at the homes surrounding the park. Grey silhouettes of three- and four-story buildings mostly and mostly inhabited by better-off inhabitants of the city. Bernie lived on a street two blocks behind these reno-vated townhouses, a neighborhood untouched by the city's decision decades ago to scoop out falling-down flophouses and small factories to make this park.

Wet snow was falling. Big globs dropping down like aliens from a great white mother ship that covered the whole sky. The trees had had their moment of glory a few weeks before. Now they were almost bare. The leaves underfoot were soggy and brown. Somewhere outside the park a persistent siren was whining. The winter dampness had a faint but depress-ing odor to it.

Bernie stood staring at the cat, which was now acquiring a soft covering of snow. His own sweatshirt was getting damp.

What to do? Leave it and hope that city maintenance would dispose of it? He really ought to finish his laps, go home and get ready for work. (This sure would be some story to tell at the office.) But it seemed somehow inhumane just to abandon a fellow mammal like a piece of trash. Shouldn't someone bury it?

"Hiya, Bernie! Whatcha looking at?" Bernie's thoughts were interrupted by a very short man. The guy wasn't five feet tall.

"I'm sorry," Bernie replied, a little flustered, "do I know you?" The new arrival was in an underwear-like sleeveless top which revealed tattoos all over him. On his feet were flip-flops with daisies on the straps. Bernie had seen him jogging in the park (Who could miss this unusual figure?) but couldn't remember ever being introduced.

"Fernwood P. Grosvenor," said the small man. "My friend Ruby told me who you were."

Ruby was another regular on the jogging circuit. Bernie didn't know her very well. He thought she was kind of nutty, and he was always uncomfortable when he bumped into her on the park path. She would stop him, greet him enthusiastically and want to engage in conversation. Her sociability was not shared by Bernie, who only wanted to finish his torture and get on with his day.

"I was on my way up to look at the crime scene," Fernwood Grosvenor pressed on. "I'm a private investigator, and I thought I might help. Here's my card," he added, pulling it out of a pocket in his shorts and shoving it towards Bernie.

Bernie didn't want the card, but he took it anyway. "Crime scene?"

"Yeah. Didn't you see the news? They found a dead guy up ahead." Fernwood pointed up the path where Bernie hadn't traveled yet.

"I haven't checked the news yet," admitted Bernie.

"Big time lawyer. Lying face down in the pond, right on the shoreline. Must've happened last night..."

Bernie shifted nervously. First the cat memorial. Now this. The day was not starting out in a promising way.

"Why'ncha come with me," suggested Fernwood. "Let's see what we can find out."

"Oh, uh, thank you, Mr...uh..." (Bernie looked at the business card. He wasn't sure how you addressed a... you know... a dwarf) "...Grosvenor. You go on ahead. I've got some business here." Bernie turned back towards the cat.

"Restroom's back there," said Fernwood pointing.

"No, I mean this cat."

Fernwood followed Bernie's gaze. "Looks dead to me."

"Yeah," agreed Bernie, "I'd leave him for the park guys to dispose of, but somebody went to a lot of trouble to make a kind of memorial."

"You'd think they'd have buried him," mused Fernwood.

"That's what I mean." Bernie put his hands in his pockets. It was really getting chilly now, and he ought to get back to dress for work. Not that he had an inspiring job. Coding. Creating uninteresting software for uninteresting apps. But despite his degree, it was the only job he could get. He'd applied for work at some of the big tech companies on the coast, but nobody seemed interested.

Well, for the time being, he had to keep his resume up, show that he was a steady, reliable worker and all that. And getting to work on time was part of it.

He looked down at the cat again, ignoring Fernwood. It had once been a beautiful animal, with golden fur now being matted by the falling flakes of snow. He couldn't just leave it here.

"I was thinking, yeah, someone ought to bury him." He looked at the cat's upturned face. Its eyes stared back unblinkingly. Bernie remembered movies where someone would place their fingers on the eyelids of a recently departed character – and gently close them. It was the least he could do for the cat.

He reached down. He couldn't find the eyelids. But he touched the eyes. They were hard as glass. In fact, Bernie began to realize with some horror, they were glass.

He moved his hand away and in doing so pushed aside one of the resting paws. On the inside of the leg, he could see big, clumsy stitches.

"Sonofagun!" Bernie said out loud. "It's a toy!" A toy, perhaps, but to Bernie it was the most life-like toy he'd ever seen. Even with the glass eyes and the matted fur, it looked like a forlorn and abandoned pet.

Fernwood moved in closer and started to poke at the inert form. "Yeah. A pretty beat-up toy I'd say. Looks like somebody tried to repair it. Look at that sewing..."

Bernie brushed away Fernwood's hand. "Maybe we shouldn't mess with it. It's like some kid was trying to say goodbye to a favorite plaything."

Fernwood put his thumbs in his running shorts. "So it's a toy. You going to leave it here after all?"

"Whaddya think?" Bernie looked at the little man. "It's kind of sad. If we leave it here, the park guys will just scoop it up and throw it in the trash."

Fernwood turned to move on up the path. "Yeah. I agree. Leave it be. C'mon. Let's go up and see what the cops found."

Bernie looked back at the cat. What an elaborate layout. Like a viewing in a funeral home. As if someone couldn't bring themselves to bury it, or give it to Goodwill. How long did it take to arrange it? And if it was a kid, why did they pick the park? Didn't want others to witness their sorrowful mission? (Kind of a public place. When did they do it? In the middle of the night?)

The more he thought about it, the more uneasy he became. It didn't seem right to just leave it.

"Hiya guys! On your way to the crime scene?"

It was Ruby, dressed in running shoes, an expensive-looking skirt and a big puffy winter jacket.

Fernwood pointed to the makeshift funeral scene. "Bernie found a toy cat."

"Well, bully for him!" exclaimed Ruby, giving a cursory look at the bushes.

Bernie went on the defensive. "It wasn't just tossed there. Somebody went to a lot of trouble to fix it up like it was a funeral. Kinda sad, you know? Seems a shame to just leave it to be dumped in the trash. I was thinking that maybe I ought to take it home and bury it or something." His voice trailed off.

"Oh come on, Bernie," huffed Ruby. "It's a toy, for crying out loud. And a pretty ratty one as far as I can tell. Let the maintenance guys take care of it. Personally, I wouldn't touch it. It might have germs." She turned to Fernwood. "You involved with that dead guy, Fern?"

"Not yet, but I'm sure the cops will want my help. I've helped them crack some cases before."

"Oh please, Fern. The only case you've ever cracked was about some guy behind in his alimony." She began striding up the path, stopped and turned...

"Good luck with your toy, Bernie," she said. "I still think you ought to let the park guys take care of it. The real tragedy is up ahead."

"Thanks for the advice," Bernie whispered as he watched the pair disappear up the path. Then he reached down, carefully wrapped the cat in the newspaper blanket and started home.

~~~~~~~~~~

Fernwood and Ruby jogged slowly up the path until they came upon yellow "Police: Do Not Cross" tape stretched across the lane. Just beyond, a group of uniformed men were busy with sundry kits and tools.

Fern called out to a tall husky man who seemed to be in charge.

"Hey, Sim! Whatareyafinding?"

The big man turned and saw the pair leaning over the police tape.

"Hiya, Fern! Sorry. Can't stop. We're kinda busy."

"Saw you on TV this morning," called Fern, ignoring the rebuff. "Big time stuff. It was Jim Cabot the lawyer, right?"

Simeon Holt, Detective Sergeant for the city, paused, with an annoyed look on his face. Fernwood Grosvenor was not simply a curious onlooker; the small man had long ago succeeded in making himself useful to the department. Frustrated by physical standards that caused his rejection as a regular policeman, he persisted in offering help, first as a volunteer and later as a frequent subcontractor. The sergeant had initially resisted Fernwood's suggestions, but the latter's high intelligence and sharp insights had eventually won him over.

Over the decades, Fern had become a good friend – sometimes irritating, but always loyal. Now, though, Sergeant Holt was preoccupied with all the details of the scene at hand, and he didn't need interruptions.

Grudgingly, he confirmed Fern's information. "James Cabot was the name in his wallet," he said, now leaning over a passel of weeds along the shore.

"So what's the verdict? Did he drown? I heard he was sort of a souse. What was he doing down in the park at night?"

Holt, anxious to cut the nagging questions short, said, "Have to wait for the coroner's report, Fern. He had a pretty big wound on his head. Somebody may have clocked him."

"Oh ho! Murder, huh? Whaddya think? Robbery?" Fernwood moved to let Ruby have a better view of the scene.

The sergeant, writing in his notebook, began to move away from his persistent interviewer. "No more questions, Fern. We'll probably have a report tomorrow. Wasn't robbery, though. Mr. Cabot had over a thousand dollars in his wallet and a lotta gold rings on his fingers. The only things missing were his shoes."

"No shoes!" Fernwood looked at Ruby. "Whaddya make of that?" He repeated the question to Sim. "Why would anyone steal shoes and leave a thousand bucks in the guy's wallet?"

But Sim was no longer paying attention. He had returned to the business around him.

Ruby tugged at Fern. "C'mon, Fern. We're in the way here."

Fernwood grudgingly followed Ruby as she turned and went back along the path. Bernie and the cat had long gone. Fern looked briefly at where the cat had been. Already, a breeze was blowing away the circle of flowers, and his mind quickly returned to the site of the dead man.

"You've heard of that lawyer, haven't you Ruby? James Harriman Cabot. Very, very smart. Very, very rich. Old family and all that. But like I said, I heard he loved his drink."

"Yeah," murmured Ruby. "I've heard of him."

2

Violet Simmonds is Bernie Zellinsky's live-in girlfriend. They met two years ago when both were participating in an LGBT protest rally. Both of them are straight but they have a lot of friends who claim alternate genders.

On this night, she came home and found a bundle on the kitchen table, wrapped in a newspaper.

"Bernie!" she had called into the next room, "What is this?"

"It's a toy cat. I found it in the Park. I'm going to bury it."

Violet began poking at the bundle. The newspaper wrapping began to unwrap. Well, yeah, it was a toy cat. A little beat up.

"Whatever made you bring this home? And why are you burying it? Why didn't you let the Park throw it in the junk?" Violet loved her sweet Bernie, but sometimes his behavior was a little odd.

Bernie sauntered out into the kitchen, holding a glass of wine.

He idly tried to recover the cat. "I felt sorry for it..." he began.

"Sorry for a bit of trash?" Violet pushed Bernie's hand away and again looked at the toy.

"It wasn't, like, trash," Bernie went on. "Somebody had laid it out like it was in a funeral home. Flowers all around it. It was really sad, like somebody making a memorial to a kid. You know, like the kid died or something."

Violet was only half listening. Gingerly, she picked up the cat. It certainly was a very real-looking toy. Must have been expensive when it was new. She lifted one of the animal's limp paws.

"Looks like somebody tried to fix it. It's sewed up. Not a very good job. I coulda done better than that." She pulled at the crude stitching, which suddenly pulled apart.

"Well, will you look at that!" she exclaimed.
Bernie did look. The cat was stuffed. With rolls and rolls of paper currency.

"Jesus, Bernie!" Violet couldn't contain herself. "We're rich!" She yanked out one of the rolls and began to peel off a sample bill. As she began to unfurl it, though, her smile turned to a puzzled frown.

"What is this? It looks like Monopoly money!" She handed the bill to Bernie, who adjusted his glasses and inspected it closely. It looked like a five-dollar bill, but it had a picture on it of an Indian, a Native American.

"Damn!" he murmured. Finding the cat and its funereal display in the Park was one thing. But finding money stuffed inside was something else. And play money? Was this some kind of unbalanced joke? Suddenly, he couldn't decide whether to call the Parks Commission, the cops or one of the local TV stations.

Violet interrupted his thoughts. Pulling another bill off the roll, she flattened it on the table.

"You know, this looks legit. The only thing really odd about it is having that Indian's picture on it. I don't know much about money (since I don't come in contact with it as often as I would like). But this is a five dollar bill, and I thought Abe Lincoln's picture was on fivers."

"It says it's a silver certificate," said Bernie, reading. "Maybe that's the difference. Or maybe they printed these before Lincoln was President."

"You mean like this is real antique money?" Violet flipped the bill back and forth in her hands. "Let me get my laptop and see if we can Google it."

The laptop was Violet's prized possession. And "possession" was the operative word. She didn't own it. The charity she worked for had loaned it to her, a small but cherished gesture that sort of made up for her meager salary. The only reason it functioned here in the apartment was that the guy downstairs had Wi-Fi and she and Bernie could piggyback on the signal.

In truth, Violet didn't "own" much of anything. She'd come to the city almost penniless and her situation now, years later, wasn't much better.

Bernie had told her he had grown up poor in a low-income section of town, the fourth oldest in a passel of eight children. Violet wondered what it would have been like to have grown up with so many brothers and sisters. She was an only child and often a lonely one. Her grandma was grim and taciturn, a woman old long before her time. Her attitude towards Violet was one of stoic tolerance. The unstated rule of the house was that the less of a burden you posed, the less likely you were to upset her.

Her grandfather was a little friendlier, although neither of the elders demonstrated what Violet might have called "love." Unlike her grandmother, though, her grandfather did talk to her, mostly when he was teaching her how to handle chores around the farm. Her grandmother didn't teach her much of anything. Any domestic skill she learned, like cooking or laundry, she picked up by observation.

She also learned that anything she needed had to be expressly requested. Nobody seemed to notice that she was constantly growing out of her clothes, nor was there any effort to register her for school. (Fortunately, when she was about seven, an aunt who lived over in the next county, paid a rare visit and asked how Violet was doing in school. Her grandfather said without apology, "She don't go to school." The aunt was quite surprised, and warned the family, "If you don't send her to school, you could get into trouble with the law!" She offered to register Violet and to arrange for bus transportation. The grandparents agreed, but didn't seem particularly appreciative.)

Violet loved school, although in the beginning, she was mocked by her classmates, because she was behind by a grade. This tapered off as her first year progressed, because she made such rapid progress. In fact, Violet's sheer determination to survive in this new environment soon made her a star pupil. The only reason she was not snubbed as a "teacher's pet" was her equally determined friendliness. Having grown up in a soulless household with no playmates, she was energized by other children and quickly developed a talent for making them like her.

Bernie had had better luck school-wise. He'd ended up getting a scholarship at the local community college, and had graduated with a degree in computer science.

The degree was not doing him much good currently, however. He was stuck in a low-paying job doing "coding." And Violet noted with some small pride, that while he had a computer at work, they didn't give him a laptop he could take home, like hers.

Now under the glare of the kitchen's overhead light, she set the laptop down on the table, opened it up, clicked on Google and quickly zeroed in on "U.S. Currency with Native American pictures." Ignoring all the coins with Indians on them, she found "The Only Native Person to Ever Grace Paper Money in the U.S." – and an exact replica of the money they were holding in their hands.

Bernie looked over her shoulder and started reading about Running Antelope, a Hunkpapa Lakota chief. The silver certificate had been printed in 1899, and the portrait was not quite authentic, since the chief had been made to wear a Pawnee headdress. This was because (legend had it) his own headdress was too tall for the painting on which the engraving was based...

"Yeah, yeah, yeah," interrupted Violet who switched to the eBay website. "Let's get down to the important things in life: How much is old Running Antelope worth?"

As Violet scrolled down the listings, they gasped. "My God!" burst out Violet. "$850! $975! Bernie! Do you realize what we have here?? They're talking about the price of one bill. We must have hundreds of them!"

God, oh shit, thought Bernie. This could be a lot of trouble.

Who left it there? Did it have anything to do with the dead guy they found up the path? A drug payoff? On the other hand, if indeed it was a memorial for some little kid, whose money was it?

"Maybe it's counterfeit," mused Bernie out loud, trying to calm the storm inside himself.

"No, no, Bernie, this is the real thing," insisted Violet. "We better get it into the bank, quick!"

"If it's real, it's not ours. We shouldn't keep it. We gotta return it."

"To who?" retorted Violet.

Good question. Boy what a mess, thought Bernie. "Well, first thing, we oughta make sure it's genuine. I've got a friend at work, Dick Hunter. He's always talking about his coin collection – and he might know something about this. He jogs in the Park like I do. I'll take one of these bills over in the morning and show it to him."

"Meantime," interjected Violet, "what should we do with the cat and all these bundles of money?"

"Hide it under the bed," said Bernie, wrapping the mysterious bundle in its newspaper blanket.

Fernwood P. Grosvenor stepped out of the shower, and while toweling himself off, looked into the full length mirror on the door. He had just returned from a jog in the park, six blocks away. Now he looked at his muscular, tattooed body, somewhat less than five feet tall.

The tattoos were a glorious gallery representing all of Fernwood's enthusiasms, from the United States of America (the national eagle emblem) to an elaborate heart embracing the name of his beloved brother Chauncey. Chauncey had encouraged and protected Fernwood all through their growing up. Unlike Fernwood, the older Chauncey was near normal size and had always fiercely defended Fernwood against all the cruel taunts and discrimination the younger man had experienced throughout his life.

Partly as a result, Fernwood had arrived at adulthood fully confident of himself. He viewed his short stature as merely a God-given "difference," a gift that he felt had been bestowed on all human beings. Except, in his case, he believed that his own difference had produced a superior human being. He was indeed a bright, enterprising man who, once people got past initial impressions, intrigued them and often found him weirdly appealing.

Besides admiring his damp body in the mirror, Fernwood was mulling over the odd events of the morning. He and Ruby had interrupted their jogging in the park to take a look at the place where some guy had been bumped off the night before. A big time lawyer. Fernwood had hoped the police would ask him for help in solving the crime, but so far, they seemed bent on dealing with it themselves.

And then there was the guy with the cat. On the way to the crime scene, he'd come across him – another jogger. Somebody that Ruby knew – Bernie – upset for some reason because he'd found a toy cat that somebody had thrown away. Fernwood's first reaction had been to suggest that the cat be left where it was, and disposed of by park personnel. But the guy pointed out that the cat had not been just thrown away. It had this whole elaborate display around it, like somebody was trying to give it a funeral or something. The guy, Bernie, thought that it deserved better than a park trashcan. He said he was going to take it home.

Well, the world is full of odd people, thought Fernwood as he revolved his small body slowly in front of the mirror. If it had been him, he would have left the cat for the park's cleanup crew. Yeah, it was a mystery, but hell, people were always leaving memorials like that around. The real mystery was up the path – the dead guy. That merited serious investigation.

Fernwood had established himself as a private investigator. Due to his unusual physical appearance, though, it was difficult to perform typical acts of a P.I. like secretly "shadowing" others. So he had gravitated towards a specialty in online projects – emails, data mining, etc.

Now as he pondered dead lawyers and toy cats, he dressed in one of his custom-made suits and headed for his office. The suit had been made to order by a tailor in China, one of five that had cost him an arm and a leg, except that Fernwood had let his credit card balance run, paying only the monthly minimum. Actually, the balance had grown pretty big, helped by the fact that Fernwood tended to postpone payment on all of his large purchases. This included the rent on his apartment and his office in the center of the city – plus all the plush furnishings he had bought for them.

Fernwood believed fervently in going First Class, whatever the event or purchase. Being the superior being he firmly considered himself to be, he thought he deserved only the best. It wouldn't hurt, though, if a nice big case came in, or if he could be assigned an ongoing investigation with a generous fee and expense account.

The "cat case" as he began to call it didn't fall into any of those categories, of course, but the next morning, as he was again jogging in the park, he bumped into the Bernie guy.

"Hiya," Fernwood greeted him enthusiastically as he caught up with the galumphing younger man. "So, how's your cat? Did you give it a proper burial?"

Bernie had to squint through his glasses before he recognized the small figure.

"Uh, no. My girlfriend found out that it was stuffed."

Well, duh, I guess most toy animals are stuffed."

"Yeah, but this stuffing was different."

"Yeah? Don't tell me. It was full of dope packets," Fernwood joked.

"No," Bernie wasn't amused. "It was money. Play money," he blurted out, suddenly realizing that he needn't have shared this info.

"Play money?!" Fernwood had to admit he was surprised. "What kind of play money? Monopoly money? That really sounds cuckoo. Who would stuff a toy with play money and leave it out in the snow?"

"I got a couple of samples here," replied Bernie, pulling some bills out of his running pants pocket. "I was hoping I'd run into a friend who jogs here like I do. He's always talking about his antique money collection, and I thought I'd show him, just to be sure it's not worth anything."

Fernwood reached over and took one of the bills. Staring at it closely, he mused, "Really, really strange. It looks like real money, but it's got a picture of an Indian on it. I've never seen anything like that. I would think if it was play money, they'd make it more fake looking, you know what I mean?"

"Yeah," agreed Bernie, reaching for the bill that Fernwood was holding. "That's what Violet and I were thinking." Bernie didn't bother to tell Fernwood about Chief Running Antelope. Instead, he said, "That's why I'm showing this to Dick."

"Wait," said Fernwood. "Could I borrow this sample? I'll bring it back. I got an expert too – down at the museum. I mean, this guy is a professor, really into antique money. I think he's written a book about it. If anybody is going to give us the real scoop, this guy will. Whadddya say?"

Bernie could not think of a reason not to let Fernwood show the bill to his expert. Another mind on the question wouldn't hurt, although he was sure that Fernwood's professor would only confirm that the currency was indeed "play money." Still, he thought, you never know. After all, Google said it was legit, and if the professor gave it the stamp of approval, he and Violet would be, in Violet's words, "rich."

As he handed the bill over to Fernwood, Bernie remembered the little man's mission on the day before.

"What did you find out about the dead guy yesterday?"

"Oh, yeah. Nothing, really. Cops were all over the place. I knew the guy. Big time lawyer. What he was doing down here in the park at night is anybody's guess." Fernwood glanced behind them and realized that they were standing next to the spot where the cat had been found.

Except that now, there was no trace of the circle of flowers that had surrounded the cat. The area had been raked over.

"Hmmm," he mused out loud. "The park guys are starting their spring cleanup kind of early. Look. No sign of Kitty's resting place."

Almost on cue, a man in a Park Service uniform came up the path, pushing a wheelbarrow with tools and a bag of ice melt in it.

"'Scuse me. Comin' through," he apologized.

"You guys are out early," observed Fernwood. "When did you clean up the bushes here?"

"Not us," said the burly man, setting down the barrow. "We don't do spring cleanup for another coupla months." Pointing to the wheelbarrow, he added, "I'm on my way to an icy patch on the path. Don't want you jogging guys to slip, you know?!"

"Well, you cleaned this up," insisted Bernie, pointing to the site of the cat's memorial. "One of your buddies must've been working overtime."

"Yesterday, there was kind of a memorial here," Fernwood added. He started to elaborate on yesterday's find, when the park employee interrupted him.

"A memorial? Man, that's kind of creepy! Close to where they found that dead guy. You don't suppose there's a connection, do you?" He shook his head again, took another swift glance at the two joggers, then picked up the handles of his wheel-barrow. "Funny, though, that somebody came along and cleaned it up."

"Whaddya think, Bernie?" Fernwood looked up at the curly-haired, bespectacled figure next to him, now scratching at the waistband of his sweatpants.

"Could all be a coincidence, I suppose," said Bernie. "But I can't figure why somebody came back and cleaned up the memorial – you know, like they didn't want it to be found. If it was me, with a murder just a few yards up the path, I'd stay the hell away from here. And I wonder what they thought when they found that the cat was gone. With all the money in it, I mean."

"Yeah," agreed Fernwood. "Makes me all the more anxious to show your Indian bill to my professor. I'll try to see him today. I'll check back with you here tomorrow, especially if he's got a clue."

The morning sun had risen and was clearing away the mist over the pond. Bernie had to hurry, or he would be late to work.

4

While strolling in the City Park, Ruby recalled her recent visit to the crime scene at the local pond. She recognized the unfortunate victim and had found herself cold and shivering. He had been her teenage lover.

Looking back on those younger days, she wondered why she had come to the conclusion that she was in love with James Harriman Cabot, her father's estate attorney. After all, she was only eighteen and he was definitely an old man. Well older. Maybe forty. Thirty at best. He was tall and strong. He had looked at her the day he arrived at the house for a meeting with her father. Never mind that he had looked at her sister in the same way. Alexandria was unmarried, thirty-two and hard at work looking for a rich husband to support her upscale desires. Anyway, after the meeting was over and the financial matters were settled, Mr. Cabot had turned to Ruby, touched her arm, and told her how pretty she looked in her pink, lacy dress. That was it! She knew she had met her one, true love. The next three months were a whirlwind of secret meetings and out-of-town rendezvous.

But the good times vanished when he no longer called. Nor did he return her desperate messages. When she realized that he no longer wanted to be with her, she fell apart with an emotional breakdown.

While she struggled with years of therapy to regain a stable life, her sister showed little compassion and continued the belittling remarks that defined her long standing jealousy of Ruby's youthful beauty.

It was after Ruby had determinedly finished business school and found a part-time job with the firm of Tyler Johnson, Landscape Architects, that she was able to take a small apartment in the lower income section of the city near the park. There she met Bernie Zellinsky and Violet. At last, she had met approval and friendship. Another acquaintance became a special friend as well. Fernwood Grosvenor was a private investigator. They often jogged together along the walking path. Ruby's dream of achieving competence and independence was realized at last.

Later, when she had met a beautiful, olive-skinned woman in the park, she knew she was welcome in the neighborhood. Maria Morningstar, who had taken a lunch break in the park, caught sight of Ruby and noticed her shabby running shoes and outdated skirt. She approached her, holding out her hand and introducing herself.

"I'm Doctor Maria Morningstar. I'm the veterinarian at the Animal Hospital. I also volunteer at the Animal Rescue League."

Ruby was impressed. She was thinking about the absurdity of the cat in a funeral display but decided not to mention it.

"My name is Ruby Rakovsky, and I run here often."

Choosing a secluded bench, they decided to sit for a few minutes under a tall cedar. Maria opened the conversation.

"I've been rather busy with my practice and have been looking for a safe place where I could jog."

"Oh yes," Ruby responded. "The park is very well patrolled. There's a security team from six o'clock in the morning until ten at night, spring, summer, fall and winter." Ruby was glad to be of help to the friendly woman with the beautiful green eyes and long coal black hair.

The doctor wanted to know more about Ruby.

"Perhaps we will see each other again along the walking path." Handing Ruby the business card she always carried, Maria encouraged Ruby to call her any time she would like to get together.

"This would be a perfect meeting place," responded Ruby.

"Hey, Rube!" A loud voice from somewhere behind the bench startled her. The women turned quickly and saw a small man in his newly purchased sports pants and casual shirt speeding towards them.

"Oh, it's only Fernwood. He jogs here too."

Fernwood approached the bench. Taking a couple of deep breaths, he asked, "Who's your friend, Ruby?"

"This is Doctor Morningstar. She's the veterinarian at the Animal Hospital, and I suspect she's the one who took care of my boss's cat when it took ill." (Maria nodded and smiled in confirmation.) Ruby went on, "What's up?"

The doctor, sensing that this would be a good time to return to her patients, stood up.

"Nice to meet you, Mr. Fernwood. See you around!" She smiled, waving as she left.

Fernwood sat down.

"How would you like to accompany me to the museum?"

Ruby hesitated. "What for?"

"To see a man about a five dollar bill. Bernie gave me a sample of the money he found in that toy cat."

Ruby frowned, questioning. "What? Money?"

"I have an appointment to see an old friend there. He is the head of the Antiquities Department and specializes in antique money. Come on, Rube. The walk will do you good." With that, he stood up, pulling Ruby up with him, and with his hand at her back, propelled her along the path to the nearby street.

Since the museum was a brisk thirty-minute walk away, he suggested they enjoy the sunshine, blue sky and snowless morning. Deciding at that point she really had no reason not to join him, Ruby readily agreed.

"Okay! Let's go!"

Walking side by side along a walkway of a footbridge above the pond, Ruby noticed a moving figure below.

"Look, Fern. There's someone skating on the ice. Wouldn't you think it's pretty stupid to take a chance like that on the pond and fool around like that?"

Fernwood moved over and glanced down. "Some people are just plain nuts."

Leaving the bridge, they took the path that crossed the University campus, reviewing the events of the past week... Ruby laughed.

"What a crazy situation! Imagine Bernie thinking he'd

found a dead cat! He's such a sentimental animal lover."

Fernwood agreed. "He's a real softy."

Conversation seemed unnecessary as the sun appeared from behind a wispy cloud, providing a bit of warmth as they quietly strolled along, unaware that they had been holding hands. They crossed the street and headed toward the museum, feeling pleasantly comfortable until they both realized they were swinging their clasped hands in time with their rhythmic footsteps. Initially embarrassed, they released their hands, neither one acknowledging the unexpected turn of events. Nevertheless, as they approached the wide marble stairs leading to the entrance doors, they were both feeling pretty good. Instinctively pausing at the foot of the long stairway, Fernwood turned to face Ruby.

"Hey Rube, I just want you to know I enjoy being with you. Thanks for coming along."

"No problem, Fern. It was great." Ruby smiled to herself as they climbed the stairs and opened the wide heavy doors. The first thing she noticed as they entered the lobby was a large black glass directory at the center of the reception foyer. She raced ahead to see it more closely. Pointing a finger at the gold-lettered listings, she read aloud, "Antiquities Department. Second Floor." Turning around to Fernwood, she called, "Let's take the elevator!"

Together they found the Antiquities Department. The door was open. As they entered, they noticed that the gray-haired man behind the desk was examining a coin with a jeweler's loupe. On the desk was his business name plate: "Samuel J. Collins, PhD."

Looking up, he recognized Fernwood.

"Oh yes, Fern! I was expecting you!" Standing at his desk,

he reached out to welcome his old friend. "And who is your lovely companion?"

Fernwood introduced Ruby, smiling at the compliment.

"Well," Collins began, "Have a seat, you two, and tell me what you have been up to lately."

The pair took the two chairs in front of the desk, while the professor returned to his seat, stretching out his long legs under the desk and clasping his hands under his chin.

Reaching into a back pocket, Fernwood produced his wallet containing a sample of the money.

"It was discovered stuffed inside a toy cat found at the City Park. No one knows how or why it was hidden there. It has become quite a mystery." With that, Fern offered the sample across the desk to the professor.

"We hope you can confirm its legitimacy and tell us something about its history."

"I should say so," hummed the professor as he examined it closely.

"Yes, yes. This is a rare find. It surely appears to be legitimate United States currency. I do recognize Chief Running Antelope of the Hunkpapa Lakota tribe. It was one of the seven Council Fires, and he was the head of the Great Circle when all the tribes would gather together. They always set up their lodges at the entry way to the Circle when the Sioux Nation met in convocation with the tribes. As a young man, he was the leader of the buffalo hunts and a brave warrior. In later years, he became a great policy and decision maker. He was known as the good friend of the white man. Yes, he was quite important in those days."

Glancing back at the portrait on the silver certificate which he was carefully holding in his hand, he sighed. He handed it back to Fernwood, who quickly returned it to the wallet, which he put back in his pocket.

"As a matter of fact," the professor finally announced, leaning back in his comfortable chair, it's a priceless antique. Museum grade, I should add."

"Oh my gosh!" Fern ecstatically exclaimed. Suddenly leaping to his feet, he lifted Ruby up, gave her a massive hug and whirled her around the room. "Just wait till Bernie gets a load of this!"

Too excited to be formal, he quickly thanked the professor, and dragging Ruby along, sped to the door. "You'll hear from me again soon, Sam. I'll keep in touch."

With that, he and Ruby swiftly disappeared down the hall and headed for home.

5

Dr. Tyler Johnson lives with his eight-year-old son Jackson, and their cat Sunshine in one of the townhouses at the edge of the park. As a young landscape architect with a highly impressive resume, Dr. Johnson had been chosen to design the park by the County Commissioners to replace an old dilapidated area that had been cleared for the project. The park would enhance the newly renovated townhouses and provide green acres for wildlife and a diversified community of city people to enjoy.

It was late autumn. Dr. Johnson and his son were lingering at the table in the kitchen after dinner. Tyler was enjoying a second cup of coffee, and Jackson was having what they referred to as coffee-sham, a cup of warm milk with two tablespoons of decaffeinated coffee mixed in. They were having a solemn discussion about Sunshine.

Three years earlier, for Jackson's fifth birthday, Tyler asked him what he would like for a gift to mark the occasion. Jackson answered, "Dad, am I old enough to have a real pet yet?"

Tyler said, "I was wondering if you might be thinking about that."

As they got into the car, Tyler said, "We will go to the Animal Rescue Center, because the pets there are so eager for a family to adopt them, love them and give them a happy place to live."

Tyler knew that his son wanted a puppy, but he suggested, "Cats are good pets for people who are away from home for a good part of the day, at work or at school. They are more comfortable being alone than dogs are and can care for themselves with responsible, caring humans who see that fresh food, water and clean litter are available."

Jackson loved and admired his dad and wanted to be just like him. Even though he had his mind set on a puppy, he decided to see some cats. So off they went to the Animal Rescue Center. As they pulled into the parking lot, they found that the building was much larger than they had expected. Inside, there were large, separate rooms, one for dogs, another for cats, and still another for "exotic" animals who were thought by some to be adorable as little ones but not so much as they grew up. There was also an area where there were display tables with items necessary for the care and amusement of adopted pets in their new homes. The last room was the office of Dr. Maria Morningstar, the veterinarian.

They stepped into the room for felines and toms. After gazing around the room for a minute, Jackson let go of Tyler's hand and made a beeline for a cage directly across the room. He sat down on the floor and was greeted by a soft "meow." The kitten's beautiful golden fur was like a ray of sunshine. Jackson was smitten by this kitten. Just then, Dr. Morningstar was passing through and seeing them, walked over.

"Would you like me to let the kitty out of the cage, so they can get acquainted?"

Jackson looked up imploringly at his dad, who said "Yes, that would be very nice. By the way, my name is Tyler Johnson." The veterinarian asked, "Are you related to Dr. Johnson of T.

Johnson Architects?"

"Yes," Johnson replied. "That's me and that's my company. My son is looking for his first real pet for his fifth birthday. It looks like he's found it!"

Dr. Morningstar motioned to Jesse, the clerk behind the desk, and asked her to join them. "Dr. Johnson and his son have decided on a pet. Would you take care of the paperwork?"

The rest was history.

Now, Sunshine had been with them for three years and was Jackson's best friend – affectionate, a good listener, who loved to play and seemed to understand Jackson's moods. But recently, Sunshine seemed to be unwell and was not eating much. A trip to the vet revealed that Sunshine had an advanced case of leukemia, and her lifetime would be cut short. Jackson was devastated.

Tyler said, "Son, the best thing we can do for Sunshine is to give her extra special, loving care, so that she will know that we understand why she cannot eat or play the way she used to. She just doesn't have the energy."

A few days later, when Tyler came home from work, Jackson asked, "Dad, what will we do with Sunshine after she dies?" It was obvious that she was very near the end of her life.

"One thing we could do," Tyler suggested, "would be to put an end to her suffering sooner. The vet could do that by an injection. It would be like putting Sunshine to sleep. She wouldn't feel a thing and we could be right beside her. The vet would tell us when Sunshine is gone, and we could stay with her as long as we wish to. Then the veterinarian would take care of her after we leave."

Jackson thought about it for awhile and said, "I would rather take care of her myself. Maybe we could find a place to bury her and have a funeral after." With much discussion about the legal restrictions against burying pets in communities like theirs, Jackson finally agreed to abide by the rules. Still, he couldn't quite let it go. He felt the need to show somehow that they loved Sunshine and always would – and the world should be made aware of her departure.

Tyler, having been through a similar experience when he was a child, knew how the death of a beloved pet can break a child's heart, but he recognized that he too was going to miss Sunshine. So, giving some thought to his son's wish, he said, "What do you think, Son, let's go for a walk in the park and look around for a place where we might set up a temporary memorial for Sunshine."

"Oh, Dad! Thank you! I have an idea too. Remember my toy cat that looks so much like Sunshine? Kitty Cat could take Sunshine's place in the memorial." Tyler thought to himself no wonder Jackson chose Sunshine at first sight for his first real live pet. They both had the same golden fur.

About a month later when the scent of winter was in the air and several inches of new fallen snow covered everything, the park looked like a live Christmas card. Some people got their cross-country skis out of storage and were defining the meandering walkways as they wandered along rolling knolls and down into dales. The pond, which had frozen solid enough for skating, was a merry-go-round of ski caps, mittens and heavy sweaters with ice skating boots to match. From a short distance, the scene was quite lovely with park lamps lighting up in the twilight time of the late afternoon. Music in waltz time wafted over from a brightly lit, two-story building just inside the entrance to the park.

Some of the skaters and skiers were headed toward the building where they could warm up with a hot chocolate or a hot toddy. The building was the final touch to the park, an addition that

Dr. Johnson had proposed two years earlier, when it took some salesmanship to convince the County Commissioners that it would be an asset for years to come and worth the financial cost. In fact, its construction would be less costly then than if they waited six months or a year or more in the future. After a little further explanation as to how the building would be used, Dr. Johnson won their support.

The first Saturday in December, a committee of regular visitors at the Parkview Café, as it was named, arrived to decorate the café for the coming Christmas and other cultural group activities such as Hanukkah, Kwanzaa and the New Year's holidays. After several hours of setting up and decorating the Christmas tree, placing balsam greenery on the mantel of the large stone fireplace, and hanging wreaths on the doors inside and outside, they all decided to stay and relax over pizza and favorite beverages. Their company was spread out over several tables.

This being the café's first year, the committee members were new to each other and just beginning to get acquainted. Among others in the gathering were Dr. Morningstar and Dr. Johnson.

Maria Morningstar, looking for a place to sit, spotted the table where Bernie, Violet, Ruby and Fernwood were sitting and walked over. Smiling, she asked, "May I join all you tired, hungry elves?" Ruby and Fernwood recognized Maria right away. Welcoming her, they introduced her to Bernie and Violet and explained how they had met in the park.

As they were relaxing and enjoying the holiday ambiance resulting from their combined decorating efforts, Tyler Johnson at another table became aware of one of the guys telling a story about finding a toy cat in the park while jogging there in November. As Tyler turned his attention to the unfolding saga, he looked over to see the two men and three women sitting at the nearby table. Only one of them was vaguely familiar, but all were nodding with interest at the relating of each incident by the narrator. Tyler was so intrigued by what he was hearing that he left his table, walked over to theirs and said, "Forgive me for interrupting your conversation. My name is Tyler Johnson. I was just sitting over there and couldn't help overhearing your story. I think I have something to add to it."

Dr. Morningstar looked up and said, "Oh, Dr. Johnson! I think we've met! Do you know these other people?" Without waiting for an answer, she introduced the group. Except for Fernwood and Ruby whom she had recently met in the park, she had only just become acquainted with the others herself.

Tyler nodded to each and turned to Maria. "I'm trying to recall. I think we met roughly three years ago, when my son found a cat at the Animal Shelter."

Three years ago! Dr. Morningstar was amazed that Tyler recalled their meeting. For a moment, she could not think of what to say, instead offering a lovely smile. In fact, she was surprised to realize that she found this handsome Afro-American rather appealing. Recovering, she asked, "Dr. Johnson, what is it that you have to add to Bernie's story? This is getting to be very interesting."

Tyler took note of her smile but was interested in Bernie's story, so he told the group about the death of his son's cat Sunshine and the memorial that Jackson was so set on having. "But," he said, "I had no clue about anything unusual about the toy. In fact, I went down that night to clean up the memorial, since it was probably against Park rules, and I was surprised to find the cat was gone."

Bernie leaned forward. " So it was you who removed the rest of the memorial! I had all sorts of crazy theories about its disappearance, since the Park guys said they hadn't touched it."

Tyler nodded and continued, "The cat was a gift from my parents when Jackson was born.

"When Jackson was three, my wife Grace died from a rare disease that once it struck, took her life very quickly."

Everyone was quiet for a minute or so.   Then Violet said, almost to herself as if thinking aloud, "Tyler, if your parents could recall where they bought the toy, perhaps it could shed some light on the mystery of its monetary stuffing."

"Thanks for the thought, Violet," said Tyler, "I'll ask them."

Then Maria spoke. "I was just thinking how interesting it is how people come together. I was wondering where to sit when the first person I recognized was Ruby and then Mr. Grosvenor. So, I asked if I could sit at your table. Bernie, I find your story fascinating, especially your discovery of the money with the picture of the Indian on it. I realize that I'm a relative stranger here, but I wonder if you would be comfortable with my visiting our local Native American community to see if anyone there might know something about the certificates. I've made some friends there through my work as a vet."

Turning to Tyler, she added, "Perhaps Dr. Johnson would like to join me, considering the revelation he just shared."

Bernie looked at Violet who gave a slight nod. "We appreciate your offer – and yes," he said as he turned to look at Tyler. "What do you think, Dr. Johnson?"

"Well, I'm no Hercule Poirot, so I'm not sure what I could add to the investigation - but I've watched a lot of his stories on TV." Everyone chuckled. Smiling brightly at Bernie and then at Maria, he continued. "Yes, I'd be pleased to accompany Dr. Morningstar."

As the group broke up, Maria said to everyone, "We'll get in touch if we find anything of interest." Then, she approached Tyler. "I need to check my calendar to see times when I would be free for this."

"I as well," said Tyler. "Let me check and email you several dates when I can be available." Pulling out a business card, he added, "Here's my email address, so you can do the same." Maria took the card in exchange for one of hers.

6

A couple of days later, Tyler Johnson entered an office supply store near his office. As he was examining the cost and details of a particular kind of paper, he suddenly looked up. His eyes widened with surprise, and he felt his pulse quicken as he spied Maria Morningstar on the other side of the counter. Her head was down, looking at different colors and styles of stationery.

Tyler cleared his throat, trying to compose himself, when Maria looked up.

"Oh, Dr. Johnson!" she smiled, also surprised. "Fancy you know what!"

"Yes, ditto," Tyler said. "What brings you here? Where's your white coat and stethoscope?"

"And where's your slide rule and blueprints?" Maria responded. Both started to laugh.

"I'm looking for some particular paper for a project at the office. Say! I just left work about 30 minutes ago, and I'm famished.

Would you care to join me someplace for supper?"

"Well....yes. But won't your family be expecting you?"

"They're accustomed to my irregular schedule from time to time. I'll text them that I'll be late – and say 'Hi' to Jackson. Meantime, think of a place you'd like and we'll be on our way."

After Tyler checked with his family, he turned to Maria.

"Is there family or someone expecting you?"

"No," said Maria, "I'm free this evening. There's a very nice, unpretentious Greek restaurant just around the corner, if you like Greek food."

"As a matter of fact, I know the place, and I do like the food. Great choice!"

Moments later, from the blue cold of December twilight, the two entered the warm, aromatic ambiance of Penelope's Place.

"Oh! It's cozy in here!" Maria breathed as they took off their coats. Tyler found a table and pulled out a chair for her. He settled himself opposite her and opened his menu. After ordering the wine, he asked, "What are you having?"

Maria scanned the menu and said, "Well, my favorite here is the Agvolemono soup. Then I think I'll have spinach pie and Baklava for dessert. What are you having?"

"Moussaka, for one. The soup sounds good too." After looking over alternatives, they settled on an order, handed their menus to the waiter and exchanged smiles.

"So, did you find a day when we could go see the Native Americans?" Maria asked.

"Actually, tomorrow is Saturday," Tyler started. "That would be a good day for me –maybe in the morning – and if you're up for it, we could look for a place to lunch."

"Tomorrow is a good day for me too," said Maria, "and listen, why don't I drive? I know the neighborhood."

They agreed on a time and place, clinked wine glasses and sat back for a moment.

"So, Dr. Maria," said Tyler, "tell me about yourself. It was good to meet you again at the Park Café. You were a great help with our cat, but beyond that, I know very little about you."

Maria smiled. She really liked this man. He had an easy manner about him, and she felt he was clearly interested in her. "What would you like to know? I grew up on a small ranch in Oklahoma, along with an older brother and a younger sister."

"Were you in the cattle business?" Tyler asked.

"We had some cows, a bull and some horses, but we weren't really in the business," Maria said, taking a sip of wine. "My mother and father are both artists, fairly well known in the area. They have a studio and give classes in art and Osage history and culture."

"Osage?" Tyler cocked an ear. "Like Osage Indians? Is that how you know people in our Native American neighborhood?"

"Well, it certainly made it easier to make friends there. My family is all Osage – for generations back."

"And what made you decide to be a veterinarian?"

"I've always loved animals, and my uncle is a vet. When I was a child I used to accompany him on his rounds. I soaked it all up. I couldn't get enough of learning about animals and how to take care of them. By the time I went to college, I knew exactly what I wanted to do."

She paused, swishing the wine in her glass. "And what about

you? How did you decide to become an architect?"

Tyler smiled. "You know, at first I wanted to be a commercial fisherman. My dad used to take me out deep sea fishing, and I thought it was the best life in the world. But when I got to college, I learned that there were other things to do, just as exciting. I wanted to try them all, but you know, there are limits. In my junior year, I had to get focused. I was into nature. That led me into landscaping, which got me interested in integrating man-made structures into the structures that God had made."

Their dinner had arrived. Tyler sniffed affectionately at the dishes. This was some kind of heaven, he thought to himself. Good food. An interesting, good-looking woman. He hadn't had this kind of feeling since his dear wife had died.

The conversation went on. Tyler revealed that his mother was a member of the Onondaga tribe in Maine and how important it was that his son knew about, and take pride in, his heritage. Maria was intrigued and happily let the moments drift by as they talked about movies and books that they liked, places they had visited and favorite spots in the city.

As they sipped coffee at the end of the meal, Tyler suddenly looked at his watch.

"Oh my gosh!" he exclaimed. "I hate to break this up, but I wanted to get home in time to tuck Jackson into bed." He wiped his mouth with his napkin and gently tapped Maria's hand. "Would you mind if I excused myself? I'll get the check on the way out. I'm really looking forward to our trip tomorrow." He stood up.

Maria, smiling and expressing understanding about the tall man's fatherly mission, stood up also. Tyler helped her with her coat, paid the check, and together they made their way out into the cool, crisp night.

At 10:30 sharp the next day, Maria in her Toyota Sienna van, pulled up in front of the building where Tyler's offices were. Rolling down the passenger window, she called out "Good morning!" to the familiar figure emerging from the building. Tyler, recognizing her, jumped into the passenger seat and greeted her.

"Maria! How are you this morning?"

As Tyler buckled himself in, Maria pulled away from the curb and into the slow moving traffic.

"I'm fine," she responded. "And you? Did you get home in time to say good night to your son?"

"Yes! And we had some fun together before we had to turn out the light."

Light snow was falling again, and Maria turned on the wipers. Tyler settled back and loosened his scarf.

"I've been thinking about this mission," he said. "How are we going to bring up our subject with your friend today? Have you thought about what you might be asking?"

Maria swerved to avoid a bicyclist who had suddenly pushed in front of her from between parked cars. "Whew! That was a close one! Yes, Tyler, I've been thinking about it. Tell me what you think of this: I have a friend, Loretta, who I met when I first came to the Animal Rescue Center. We became close friends. Loretta is sometimes called 'Ancient Woman' due to her advanced age – probably over a hundred, plus or minus a year or two. When I first met her, she had brought in her 14-year-old, 57-variety, mixed breed dog that was at death's door. Loretta didn't want Tonto to suffer any longer and I helped her to say farewell.

"Even though Loretta and I are good friends, I don't want to expose our other friends to curiosity seekers and fodder for gossip. So, I propose a simple, friendly visit – I haven't seen her in awhile – and save our question for last. We don't have to tell her all the history. We could just say our curiosity was prompted by a friend who had found what looked like play money with a picture of a Native American chief on it - and we just wanted to know more about how an Indian's picture got on what appears to be U. S. currency."

"Sounds like a good way to go," said Tyler. "You never know what will come up in a conversation like this...As you suggest, it's probably better not to let the cat out of the bag, so to speak." He chuckled.

"And who knows," agreed Maria, "Coming from way back, she might have knowledge of something interesting that we could take back to our friends."

City plows had done a credible job of removing snow from main streets, but after about 20 minutes, Maria turned off onto a street that had not yet been cleared. Maria drove carefully for about two blocks until she found a parking spot. Tyler followed her as they crossed the street to a brick row house.

Instead of immediately ringing the doorbell, they waited outside. Maria explained that in Native American culture, this was considered good manners. After a minute, the door opened, revealing a tiny bent figure wrapped in a hand-woven shawl.

"Hello, Loretta," Maria greeted the old woman, who looked back in pleased surprise. "We stopped for a minute to say hello. I tried to call you but I never got an answer."

"Oh Maria! How wonderful to see you!" Loretta said, extending her arms. "Come in! Come in! My phone hasn't been working for weeks. I sent a letter to the company, but I haven't heard back." She ushered the pair into the house, steering them into a front room she called her winterized "porch."

Maria introduced Tyler who was greeted with a mock look of awe. "My!" said Loretta, "You are a very tall man!" They all laughed. Loretta took their coats and insisted that they have tea, bringing them cups in shaking hands. All round them were beautiful pots with flowers growing in them. There was a handmade rug on the floor and handmade baskets sitting on shelves and tables. Tyler wanted to know if Loretta had made these items herself.

"Yes, Tyler, I made them all," said Loretta. "Over the years."

"They're very attractive, Loretta."

"I'm glad you like them, Tyler. I'm very proud of them," said Loretta. "And I've enjoyed living with them for a long time."

The two women chatted on about shared friends, about their families and the weather, about Loretta's health (aches and pains and dimming vision) until Maria casually raised the subject of their visit. She described the money in detail from what she could remember from seeing Fernwood's sample at the Parkview Café.

Loretta listened intently, but when Maria asked her if she could shed any light on the money or the Native American pictured on it, Loretta demurred.

"How interesting," she commented. "I know about Indians pictured on coins like the penny and the nickel – I think I have a bunch of them saved up somewhere..." She looked at a hutch in the corner... "but I've never heard about one pictured on paper money."

The three continued on for a moment, agreeing that such a currency was certainly an oddity and then shifting to other topics. Loretta offered more tea, but Maria said, "Thank you,

Loretta, but I really think it's time for us to leave." She stood up, then leaned over her small friend, to give her a hug.

Loretta gave her a kiss and said, "I'm so delighted that you stopped by! Such a treat to see you after all these months, and I hope you'll come again before too long. Tyler, you're always welcome. I hope you'll come again too. I'd like to get to know you better!"

Tyler grasped the small hand and told Loretta how much he enjoyed meeting her. Retrieving their wraps, he helped Maria on with her coat.

With some effort Loretta stood also, to escort her visitors to the door. As they reached for the latch, she put her finger to her cheek and said, "You know, someone who might know about your money is Alexander Rakovsky. Do you know him?"

Both Maria and Tyler looked at each other and nodded. Maria said, "The philanthropist? Didn't he die recently?"

"Oh, how sad!" said Loretta. "I hadn't heard. You know, he was very helpful when my friends and I were moved here to make way for that new park." Tyler swallowed but didn't remark on his connection to that project. Nor did Maria.

Loretta went on. "Mr. Rakovsky was very interested in Native American culture, and he used to visit us often, looking for artifacts and mementos. When the city moved us to this neighborhood, he put up some money for some of us who were, well, destitute. I don't think I could have afforded this nice house if it hadn't been for him."

"Oh, Loretta," said Maria, patting her friend's hand. "You never told me that story before! I don't want to be nosey, but how are you doing now? Do you need anything?"

"Oh no!" chuckled Loretta. "Mr. Rakovsky got me over the

initial hump, if you know what I mean. I'm doing fine now, what with my Social Security and whatnot. I needn't have brought it up, but I was just remembering how interested he was in everything about our culture and history.

Then, with a few more goodbyes, Tyler and Maria found themselves outside in the gently falling snow and carefully made their way across the street.

Maria was about to open the door of the van when she stopped in anguished surprise. "God, who did this??!!" she choked as she ran her finger along a rough gouge that extended from one end of the car to the other.

"Somebody has key-scratched you," observed Tyler as he bent close to examine the damage.

"Is that your car?" called a voice behind them. They turned to find a young man standing in the middle of the street. His hair was in a ponytail and he was wearing a soiled headband. Over his short-sleeved shirt he wore a shaggy fur vest which just reached his ragged jeans.

Maria squinted. "Is that you, Bear?" Kicking Bear, tall and handsome despite his soiled clothes, responded with a grin.

"Yes, it's me, and I see somebody has spoiled your beautiful car!"

"Yes, and it's nothing to smile about. Do you have any idea who would do such a thoughtless thing?" Maria asked the question rhetorically, already sure she knew the answer.

"Ah no," said Kicking Bear, still smiling and moving closer. He smelled. "Perhaps it was some patriot who didn't like expensive cars bearing foreigners invading our neighborhood."

"Foreigners?" asked Maria.

"Oh please!" said Bear with mock astonishment. "I know who you are. 'Doctor' — the uppity killer of innocent animals posing as a good Samaritan!"

Maria, gritting her teeth, turned to Tyler, explaining, "I think he's remembering my helping Loretta put her dog to sleep." Turning back to Kicking Bear, she said, "Bear, I'm sorry to see that you haven't changed one bit. You're still the gross, insulting person you always were!"

"And you're still the Osage Witch, traveling with all those highfalutin snobs who kicked us out of our homes so you could have your nice park. Now you're down here, pretending to be one of us 'Indians'! What are you doing here anyway??"

Tyler, upset at this vagabond ranting at Maria, took a step forward. "We are down here visiting one of the doctor's friends. We had a lovely visit and were also asking her help with questions we had."

"What kind of questions?" Kicking Bear leaned towards Tyler.

"None of your business," interjected Maria.

"I'll bet you were seeing old Loretta, that crone," smiled Bear. "She's the biggest blabbermouth on the block. Can't believe a word she says!"

"As a matter of fact," said Tyler, "she wasn't able to help us."

"'Wouldn't' help you is more like it," retorted Bear. "She may have a big mouth, but she doesn't share anything with niggers!"

"Bear!" Maria interjected, "Wash your mouth! You just insulted Dr. Tyler Johnson, one of the most respected men in the city!"

"Oh ho!" said Kicking Bear, taking a step backward and putting his hands on his hips. "The famous Dr. Johnson, Architect of the mass removal of innocent First Americans!"

"I didn't..." started Tyler, but Bear interrupted him.

"Do you have any idea of the desecration you caused??!! These people, my people, were here long before you or your slave masters ever set foot on this sacred ground. I myself am the descendant of a mighty warrior of the Lakota Sioux – a man who fought bravely for his birthright while your ancestors accepted their role as nothing more than animal labor!"

Tyler bit his lip and looked Bear up and down, his eyes finally landing on the Indian's footwear. Even snow-covered they were fine examples of a cobbler's expertise, made of fine leather and exquisite tooling. Tyler shifted his stare to Kicking Bear's eyes.

"Are those fine shoes part of the costume of a great warrior's descendant?" he asked sarcastically.

Kicking Bear bristled. Using one of his snow-covered feet, he kicked slushy white stuff onto the doctor's tailored pants. "And where, Doctor Nigger, did you get your shoes??"

Tyler, realizing that he was stooping to a crazy man's level of discourse, turned and opened the car door for Maria. Bear suddenly pulled his knife out of its sheath and jammed it into the shiny metal of the car. Tyler pulled out his cell phone.

"Please move away from the car, Bear, or I'm calling the police."

Bear stood motionless for a moment, his arm still extended, still holding the knife against the car. Then, just as suddenly as he had removed it, he returned the knife to its sheath. With cars skidding around him, he backed out into the street, turned and was gone.

On the way home, Tyler and Maria were at first silent. Maria broke the quiet.

"Boy! Fixing that scratch is going to cost a pretty penny!"

Tyler, his cool only now beginning to return, answered, "How do you know that guy? He really was scary." Maria explained that she'd been a frequent visitor to the community, both before and after they were removed to their present neighborhood. She'd gotten to know pretty much everyone who lived there, including Kicking Bear — a long time character whose neighbors tried to tolerate him, much as some old-time tribes used to indulge mentally disturbed members as "children of God."

They reviewed the events of the day, starting with their visit with Loretta. Was there any truth to Kicking Bear's claim that the old lady had held back information? Did she really know more than she was telling? Or was she sincere in suggesting that Alexander Rakovsky might have been a good resource (and if so, how might they access it now that he had passed on?)

Maria felt somehow that she had to apologize for their unfortunate meeting with Kicking Bear, but Tyler brushed it aside, saying that he hoped the loopy young man would not be a feature of any future visits to the neighborhood. As for the insults, he said he was used to them and tried to tell himself that those who uttered them had more of a problem than he did.

It did, however, remind him of the shoes Kicking Bear had been wearing. Tyler was style conscious enough to know that they were not merely "better" shoes but quite possibly custom made. Where would somebody like Bear get shoes like that?

When they pulled up in front of Tyler's condo, they agreed to keep on thinking about the events of the day and to ponder next steps. Meantime, they made a date for another supper together.

7

Bernie's passion was his collection of cheap wines. As he stood before the old glass-faced cupboard in his small kitchen, he stared at the carefully arranged row of stemware. Reaching up, he opened the door and selected his souvenir set of four, acquired at the local antique shop around the corner. (Bernie's word for it was the "Junk Emporium.") All four glasses were imprinted with the name of a famous resort somewhere in the mountains. Bernie grinned, wondering whether he would ever be lucky enough to actually stay at the resort one day. As he set the glasses on the card table at four separate places, he heard the doorbell ring. He looked up to see Fernwood opening the unlocked door.

"Hey, Guy!" Fernwood called as he traipsed from the front room and ambled toward the kitchen. "Ruby said she'd be over too." Spotting the glassware, he beamed. "Ready to celebrate, I see." He pulled out a chair and sat down while Bernie turned to his newly purchased oak wine rack on the counter and singled out two bottles.

"Which do you prefer, Fern, red or white?"

There wasn't time to answer as they were both startled by a sudden shout from the door. "I'm here! I'm here, all you lucky people!" Ruby burst into the room with all her usual trademark exuberance. "Hey! Where's Violet?"

"Oh, she's just getting dressed," Bernie replied as Fernwood examined the labels on the bottles.

"Well, here's some cheese and crackers and strawberries." Ruby set a plastic plate carrier on the table, unzipped it and removed a china serving plate filled with finger foods. "I thought we could pretend we were rich and having a congratulation party." She covered her mouth with her hand. She couldn't help giggling.

"Who are we celebrating?" Violet, dressed in her best jeans and polo shirt, stood in the entrance of the kitchen. "And what did I get all dressed up for anyhow?"

Fernwood stood up. The other three pulled out the chairs in the crowded corner of the tiny room and sat down.

"I have good news and bad news," Fernwood announced.

"Let's hear the good news first," Violet demanded.

Fern nodded in agreement. Clearing his throat, he began. "Well, I called you together to make an announcement. Ruby and I have just got back from a visit with my friend at the museum and..."

Bernie interrupted. "Get on with it, Fern. Just tell us what happened. Is our money worth something or isn't it?"

Fern hesitated. "Okay, well, yes it is."

Violet screamed, "I knew it! I knew it! We're rich! We're rich!"

"Oh Vi," Bernie interrupted again. "Get over it. Maybe there's a catch. Okay, Fern, what's the bad news?"

Ruby saw a chance to take a turn, so she charged in with an explanation. "Although the money is legal tender, it's only useful to a collector or something. That's as far as we got."

The corners of Violet's mouth turned down and she stuck out her lower lip. "Okay, what do we do now?"

Fernwood spoke up. "I guess it's up to us to find a way to transform the silver certificates into usable legal tender. I'll call Collins and see what sources he might have."

Bernie broke in. "We'll have to Google it again and see what comes up. Vi is a champ on her laptop. If anyone can find a way, she can!"

"Okay, Bernie," said Violet, "you're the idea man. We'll check it out tonight!" She was glowing at his compliment to her.

Bernie stood up. "Let's drink to that. The wine's on me."

Bernie uncorked the bottles while the other three celebrants wondered indeed how easy would it be to transform the certificates into "real" money.

After a moment, Ruby broke the silence with a change of subject.

"I consider you guys my friends," she began, "so I want to let you in on something very private. You don't know this, but I'm a lifelong member of Alcoholics Anonymous."

Fernwood was surprised. "Does that mean you can't join us in a toast?"

"I'm sorry to say I can't, but I'm happy too, 'cuz I haven't had a drink in fourteen years." Sighing, she leaned back in her chair.

Bernie, uncorked bottles in hand, stopped. "I never would have guessed, Ruby, but I'm very proud of you, especially because you trust us and consider us your friends."

Ruby smiled. "Thank you, Bern." Violet, seated on her right, put her arm around Ruby's shoulder. "Me too," she said.

Meanwhile, Fernwood, on Ruby's left, was slightly shaken. He touched her arm, nodding in a sign of agreement. Violet rose, opened the refrigerator, pulled out a can of ginger ale, and poured a glass for Ruby. Picking up a glass for herself, she said, "I'll have white, Bern..."

The men chose red wine. Bernie poured. They raised their glasses, clinking them together as Ruby made a toast.

"Skoal!" she declared with a broad grin.

As the afternoon wore on, the friends chatted and enjoyed Ruby's finger foods until it was time to go.

Fernwood walked Ruby home from the meeting at Bernie's. Ruby decided to tell him about her sister and the party Alexandria was planning for her aristocratic acquaintances.

"Fern, I told her I would be glad to supervise and help in the kitchen with the hors d'oeuvres and the dinner. I won't be joining the guests. Alexandria considers me an outsider, now that I've got out on my own. She never did like me very much anyway. I think she first considered me lower class when I started drinking. I was eighteen then."

Fernwood stopped her. "Are you sure you want to share this with me?" Ruby nodded. "Yes, I'm sure."

"Well, you can count on me to keep it to myself," Fernwood assured her. "But I'm confused. What started you drinking anyhow?"

"Well," Ruby confessed, "I had a bad experience with a man I fell in love with."

"You don't have to go on, Ruby." With that, he gave her a hug. "I'm just glad you are who you are." They said goodbye as she unlocked her door and stepped inside.

Fernwood stood for a moment in the gathering gloom, thinking about what Ruby had just told him. Then he turned away from the door and whistling a brisk tune, approached the sidewalk, jogging the rest of the way home.

~~~~~~~~~~

Two weeks later, Ruby was in the kitchen at her sister's luxurious apartment in the condos near the park. The hostess and four guests were gathered in the cathedral ceiling great room where the butler was serving the drinks while Ruby arranged hors d'oeuvres on a silver tray.

"I love doing this kind of work. I learned the culinary arts by working in a four-star restaurant to help pay my way through business school." Ruby turned to face the chef who was stirring the Vichyssoise in a large stock pot at the iron stove. The chef was impressed. "I too love creating special meals for people who appreciate my work." He winked, raising his hand and curling his fingers in the sign meaning "okay."

The butler arrived to exchange the wine platter.

"I'll refill the wines for you," Ruby volunteered. "We'll be serving dinner shortly." The butler nodded in approval as he picked up the hors d'oeuvres and left.

Turning to the chef again, Ruby offered her assistance. "I'll be glad to help plate the dinner courses for you while our butler is serving in the dining room."

"The salad, soup, entrees and desserts are all ready and holding," the chef assured her.

When the butler returned, Ruby reviewed with him the simple seating plan which Alexandria had carefully prepared. "There are four guests and the Vanderhoffs. Our host, Baron Vanderhoff, will of course be at the head of the table. His back is here at the door as you enter. On his right is Dr. Maria Morningstar. On his left is Mrs. Collins. Mrs. Vanderhoff will be at the other end of the table, facing the Baron. On her right is Dr. Samuel Collins and on her left is Dr. Tyler Johnson."

"Don't worry, Ma'am," the butler responded, "It will be a pleasure to serve this group. We've had many dinners here. I really appreciate your assistance."

Later, Ruby took her place at the doorway and signaled to Alexandria.

"Dinner is served," the hostess ceremoniously announced, leading her guests into the dining room. She busily directed them to their seats and was the last to sit down. "I want to welcome you here to our humble domicile, and now that you've met one another, I hope you will all enjoy yourselves tremendously and know how pleased we are that you are able to join us here for another of my candlelight soirees." With a bright smile, a dramatic blink of her heavily mascaraed eyelashes, a flick of her head and a quick wave to the butler awaiting her sign at the doorway, Alexandria embarked on her carefully detailed, five-course dinner party.

The dinner guests seated themselves, the gentlemen holding chairs for the ladies. Alexandria stood by her place at the far end of the table. "Now that everyone has had a chance to get acquainted, I would like to say a few words about my husband while you partake of the first course."

The Baron looked up, a quizzical look on his face, as Alexandria pressed on.

"Now that you've met my husband, Baron Walter Vanderhoff, I'm sure you've observed his retiring nature, but I must add that he is modest to a fault."

The Baron cleared his throat and started to protest. "My Dear, I don't think our guests want to hear..."

Alexandria ignored him. "Therefore, I would like you to know of his illustrious history."

The guests quietly enjoyed their Vichyssoise while Alexandria continued her declamation. "My husband has researched and patented important new discoveries in his field. His family, still residing in Vienna, are all research scientists as well and hold important government positions there."

"I'm sure you all want to know how we met," she went on. "Well, we were both board members of the country club. I must confess that it was love at first sight." Alexandria smiled proudly.

"I did not know then of the importance of his work or that he travels the world over to present his papers at international symposiums. We are indeed fortunate that he is presently associated with our beloved University and that he has been welcomed as graciously as a fellow academic."

As Alexandria paused, there were murmurs of polite agreement around the table. The soup bowls were removed and the salad was served. Conversation resumed. Alexandria joined in as she turned to Dr. Collins on her right.

"Dr. Collins, I'm so glad you were able to attend our candle-light soiree. I've been anxious to meet your lovely wife. I have to tell you that I'm impressed with the courses you offer at the university. I'd like to go with you on your next trip."

Collins smiled. "You're quite welcome to come along."

His wife chimed in. "My husband's class usually journeys out to Black Rock. Sometimes, I go along too and find a new stone for my jewelry-making."

"Mrs. Collins," interrupted Dr. Morningstar, "I would also like to come along with you. One of my father's hobbies was designing jewelry with turquoise and other precious stones. When I was a child, I watched him polish them after they were cut."

Tyler perked up. "I have a beautiful turquoise watch. I acquired it when we were traveling out west. On the back is the signature of the Native American who created it."

Alexandria entered the discussion. "I prefer diamonds myself." Conversation stopped. There was a prolonged silence. Polite conversation continued as the dinner courses were served. Then, Phoebe Collins broke in: "Is there any new news about the murder in the Park?

I heard about it at card club. They said the victim was a high powered lawyer. They found a bloody injury on his head, but it was a mystery how he ended up in the water and drowned. There was a lot of talk about it at the Country Club. They say he was a ladies' man."

Alexandria, intent on getting more information, asked, "Do they know who he was?"

"His name was Cabot, James Cabot," Baron Vanderhoff added. "Of course, I only know what was in the paper. The police are investigating, but the murderer hasn't been found yet."

Alexandria was in shock. "Oh no! Mr. Cabot was my father's

attorney. Why didn't you tell me about his death?"

Annoyed by her accusation but controlled, Vanderhoff replied, "How was I to know you knew him? You never told me. Why don't you read the paper?" Alexandria tossed her head, shrugged her shoulders and tightened her lips.

Wanting to get Tyler's attention, Samuel Collins leaned across the table to face the architect. "Some mighty strange things have been happening in the park lately. I assume the park service is on to them."

Tyler asked, "You mean, in addition to the murder?"

"Well, first this murder and then there was this couple. Came into my office last week with a story about finding a stuffed cat in the park."

"What's so strange about that?" Tyler asked.

Collins took another sip of wine, leaned closer to Tyler and whispered loudly, "It was stuffed with money."

Tyler's eyebrows arched. "Oh? Who was the couple? I think I know who you're talking about. I heard the same story the other day. You say the cat was stuffed with money?"

Collins sat back. The wine was making him dizzy. He never could hold his alcohol, even a small amount. "You heard this story? I don't know if you would know these people. They are not associated with the university. One is a long time friend of mine. Unusually short."

Collins was beginning to slur his words as the butler refilled his wine. The entrée course was nearly over and the dessert was ready to be served. "The woman wash short too. My friend introduced her. Don't remember her name. Roshy or Ruby. Shumthing like that."

On hearing the name Ruby, Alexandria sat up and cast a look at the kitchen door. Collins took another swig. Tyler stared at the professor, whose eyelids were beginning to droop. He suspected that Collins' visitors were Fernwood and Ruby. Was Collins the "friend" that Fernwood had mentioned at the café?

"Did they talk about the money in the cat, these friends of yours?"

The others at the table couldn't help hearing.

"Was it real money?" Tyler asked

"It wash very, very old," Collins responded. "Now, don't pash this on." He drew his chair up closer. "The shtory was bizarre. Quite extraordinary." Smiling, he gulped down the last of his wine.

Tyler drew in a sharp breath. "What happened to the cat?"

"Don't know."

Tyler was persistent. "Tell me more about the couple who came to visit you at your office."

The butler served more wine with the dessert course. Collins looked up, recognizing that all eyes were on him, waiting for his answer. Lifting his goblet as if for a toast, he then emptied it. "The people were friends of mine. Well, one of them anyway. The other I guesh wash hish girlfriend. Don't remember her name," he said again, now feeling the effect of the wine.

Impatient, Tyler interrupted the story. "What was the man's name? Maybe I know him."

Collins, feeling dizzy, nearly fell off his chair. "Why?" still slurring his words, "Sho why...do you...want to know...hish name?"

"No reason," Tyler sat back in his chair. "Just forget about it.

It doesn't matter." But he didn't intend to forget it. ("I'll find out somehow," he thought.) As they enjoyed their dessert, Tyler tried to appear unconcerned. He had obviously drawn the attention of the others.

Collins, feeling that he had talked too much and angry with himself, thought "I'll have to tell Fernwood that this jerk seemed a little too interested. Made me pretty uncomfortable." Looking around, he muttered, "Now wheresh that butler? I'd like more wine."

Phoebe Collins, aware that her husband had had one too many, kicked him under the table. Collins, thinking that the kick came from Tyler, jumped up, intending to toss water across the table on Tyler. He and his chair fell backward. Alexandria, feeling faint, dropped her head down on the table, barely missing the Baked Alaska. Collins was soaking wet but unhurt. The butler tried to assist him, but Collins waved him off. "Go away. I don't need you now," he complained.

The dinner party was over as the guests quickly rushed to bid farewell and get their own coats and scarves. The butler made his way to open the door while the crowd made a hasty retreat. Vanderhoff, in disgust, retired to his room without so much as a nod to Alex, who was finally getting up from the table, too distressed to say goodbye to her company.

While the butler cleared the table and returned to the pantry, Alexandria marched into the kitchen. She suspected that it was Ruby who was the girlfriend in Collins' office. Her face was scarlet. "What business was it for you to go see one of my important acquaintances?"

Ruby, in the middle of putting dishes in the dishwasher, looked up, surprised. Alex bore on. "Can't you mind your own flimsy, slimy business and leave my friends alone?"

Ruby was baffled by the onslaught. She had come to help her

sister, anticipating a long term plan to soothe the relationship between them. Since she was in the kitchen, she had not heard the conversation in the dining room.

The chef, sensing a showdown, left to join the butler.

Alex pressed on. "You thought I didn't know what you were doing with Cabot. He was MY friend until you sashayed into his life and took him away from me."

Tears welled up in Ruby's eyes. Her shoulders trembled. "Alex, I was only eighteen. He led me on..."

Before Ruby could continue, Alex interrupted. "Oh yes. You thought I didn't know about your disgusting behavior. You were a slut. He wanted ME but I turned him down. He wasn't GOOD enough for ME."

The chef appeared at the kitchen door. "I'll be leaving now, Mrs. Vanderhoff. I hope you were happy with the dinner." Embarrassed, he scurried out, making a beeline for the back door.

The butler, finishing his duties in the dining room and pantry, stopped to thank Ruby for her help. "I'll call a cab for you, Miss." He too made a fast getaway. Ruby placed the last dish in the dishwasher and sat down at the table to regain her composure.

Alexandria wouldn't be deterred. Standing over Ruby, she continued, "I hope you're satisfied. You've humiliated me in front of everyone. You've always messed up things for me. You're still a sniveling brat. Just have to get your own way."

Ruby, teary eyed, pulled out a handkerchief from her pocket. She wiped her eyes as she mustered her courage. "That's a lie," she shot back. "It was you. So happy to tell everyone that I didn't like you. Just to get sympathy. But it was a lie. Mother and Dad loved me. That made you jealous. I'm not the stupid kid I used to be."

"Oh no? You're still as crazy as you were then. I was their FIRST child. Fourteen years later, YOU were a mistake!" Alex screamed, "An accident!"

Ruby was breathing so deeply she could hardly talk. "No, no!" She caught her breath. "So mean and nasty." She caught another deep breath. "You still are." Her face was wet with tears and she dabbed at her eyes and nose.

There was a sudden, loud ring. It was the doorbell. Ruby stood up.

"That's my ride. Goodbye, Alex." Ruby tried to compose herself. "You won't have to see me again. You can't hurt me anymore." She ran to the closet, grabbed her coat and purse, opened the door and raced down to her cab.

Alexandria in pain clutched her chest, chasing after Ruby to the open door, screaming at the top of her lungs, "I hate you! I hate you! I hate you!" Then louder, "Bitch, bitch, bitch!" Slamming the door shut, she leaned her back against it, slumping in exhaustion. She whispered, "That's right, Ruby, don't come back. I don't ever want to see you again."

8

Bernie stuck his key into the lock of the apartment door. Hmmmph? It was already unlocked. Was Violet already home? (She usually got home 30 to 60 minutes after he did.)

"Violet? "he called out as he pushed the door open.

Inside was more of a surprise. Everything in the room was topsy turvy. Sofa cushions on the floor, drawer in the side table pulled out. Papers strewn all about. He went into the kitchen. Same chaos. Refrigerator door open. Cupboard doors ajar, contents spread out on the counters or on the floor. Bernie stepped gingerly around the mess and looked into the bedroom. Bedclothes ripped off the bed, bureau drawers upside down on the floor...

Instinctively, he dropped to his knees and looked for the dark corner under the bed where he had hidden the toy cat. Crap! It had been moved. Not gone. Moved. He reached out, retrieved the toy and stood up. Man, this was really strange. The money was still in the cat. If they'd been robbed, the thief had overlooked the most valuable thing in the house.

Bernie lit a cigarette and poured a glass of wine from the bottle that had been shoved to the back of the kitchen counter. After a minute, he began to pick up some of the mess. Closed the fridge and oven doors. Picked up jars off the floor. Then he stopped. If they called the cops, they would be told not to touch anything. Evidence, you know. Like clues. Or whatever.

The door opened. It was Violet. She stopped short, just as Bernie had, then spied him in the kitchen door. "What the h...???"

"We've been burglarized," said Bernie. "I was going to clean it up, but I got to thinking the cops would want us to leave everything alone."

"My god, my god," Violet started murmuring under her breath. She set her laptop on the cushionless sofa and started moving towards the bedroom.

"The cat's all right," Bernie interrupted her. "I got it here in the kitchen, and the money's still in it, would you believe?"

Violet stopped in mid-stride, turned and absently picked up a sofa cushion to return it to its place. Then she joined Bernie in the kitchen. Arms akimbo, she surveyed the damage. "Boy, they didn't miss anything did they?" Her breathing was labored.

"They missed the cat," said Bernie, handing her the toy.

Violet squeezed the toy and pulled open the wound in its under-side. Fingering the contents, she pulled out a roll of the Indian currency. She poked around some more.

"Well, they left us something," she said slowly.

"Yeah, can you beat it?" said Bernie. "They must have seen what was in there, but they left it behind."

"Not all of it," said Violet.

"What do you mean?"

"Look for yourself. There were a half dozen rolls stuffed in there. And now there's only three."

Bernie reached over and took the cat. Poking his finger into the toy, he pulled out a couple of rolls in addition to the one Violet was holding.

"Boy, that's one for Ripley. Whaddya think?
They were interrupted in the middle of swiping it?"

"Could be," Violet mused. "But why didn't they just take the cat with everything in it?"

Bernie poured himself another glass of wine.

"Think we ought to call the police?"

Violet took the rolls from Bernie and stuffed all three back in the cat. What could the police do? If they got into the act, it would just mean everybody in the world would know about the money. One burglary was enough. Once the media broadcast the news, there would be a long line at the door waiting to break in...

"What about your friend, the dwarf?" she said out loud. "Isn't he a private investigator? What about letting him in on this? He already knows we have the money. Maybe he could do some snooping around – keep it all, you know, private??"

Bernie put down his glass. "He's not really my friend. He's just a guy who jogs in the park. Well, you met him. Whaddya think?"

"I just don't like the idea of noising it around that we have all this valuable cash...which reminds me: Before anybody takes any more of it, maybe we should put it in a bank or something."

"You mean, like a safe deposit box?"

"Yeah. You have a bank account. Do they have those at your bank?"

"I guess so. But, Jeez, it's way across town. I set up my account when I was still living at home. But I hardly ever go there. Never have enough money worth depositing – and there sure isn't enough money in the account to bother getting it out..."

"Why don't we take the cat money over there tomorrow," Violet said. "I don't want to spend another day worrying whether somebody is going to break in while we're gone." She paused. "Maybe after we deposit it, we could put a note on the door that says in big letters NO MONEY."

Bernie smiled, in spite of himself. "Just our luck that the first burglar who sees that sign can't read."

Violet stuffed the cat into her backpack, announcing that she would sleep on the pack that night. Pouring herself a drink, she mused, "If we go to your bank, I'll get to meet your family."

"Oh God," Bernie groaned. "Better we should throw ourselves off a cliff!"

Violet swirled her wine. "Bernie! What a way to talk! I've never met your family. I want to see where you grew up. I never had a family except for my grandparents – and that's not really the same. You had brothers and sisters!"

"Yeah. And you can't imagine what a curse that was."

"Oh, come on, Bernie. You haven't even spoken to them since I came to live with you. They must think you're dead!"

"Goody goody for them! Goody goody for me!"

But Violet was persistent. She thought, this is ridiculous. Whatever strains and frustrations there were growing up, now is not then. Everybody is older and wiser. "Let's at least go see if they've mellowed," she summed up.

Bernie finally conceded. "But just for a minute. Poke our heads in the door, say 'Hi' and we're outa there, okay?" He was tired, and the wine had made him even sleepier. He longed to clear up the mess in the apartment, have supper and go to bed.

The next morning was Saturday. Wind whipped an icy snow against the windows. They layered themselves with sweaters, found scarves and put on their puffy winter parkas. Violet patted the cat inside her backpack as they pulled the door closed.

They took the bus, and even though it was not a workday, it was crowded. Where were all these people going? All stuffed in there with their heavy outerwear, and everybody seemed to have some enormous something to carry. Backpacks, suitcases, guitars. Some kid with a pair of skis that would knock somebody every time he turned around.

"We probably should have invited the kid's father to come with us," said Violet who had taken advantage of a seat miraculously vacated right next to her. "After all, the money is probably really his."

Bernie looked down at her. He regretted going out in this weather, and the jumble of humanity around him wasn't making him any happier. "That's a matter of conjecture," he started. "He didn't know the money was in the cat, and his father didn't know either. And, remember, they abandoned it in the park. I'm no lawyer, but I would say that they gave up all claim to the cat."

Violet was only half listening. "What'll we say when they find out that half the money is gone?"

"How do they know 'half' the money is gone? No one ever told them how much money was in there at the beginning. For all they know, what's in there now is all there ever was."

Bernie pulled the cord for the next stop, and they wrestled their way out into the blustery snow. Mittened hands in their pockets, they bent forward for the two-block walk to the bank.

Despite the weather, the bank was crowded, and it was a good 45 minutes before they finally emerged. "Are you sure you want to stop at my house?" asked Bernie hopefully, licking a snowflake off his lips. "It's over two blocks from here."

"Yes!" said Violet laughing and grabbing his arm, snuggling up close so that Bernie was forced to put a protective arm around her. Once again they bent into the swirling snow.

"Just don't mention the money or the cat," said Bernie. "Please."

It was a brick row house, with steps leading up over a basement apartment. Still battling the wind, they climbed the steps and rang the bell.

After a minute the door was opened by a short round woman with white hair haphazardly pinned up.

"Bernie!" she cried, hand at her breast.

"Hi, Ma. This is Violet."

"Come in! Come in! Oh my stars!" She turned as they entered and called back into the house.

"Everybody, come! Come! You'll never guess who's here!"

"Oh my God in Heaven, Bernie!" She reached up, hugged him tightly and kissed him on both cheeks. "It's a miracle! It's been so long!! I worry about you every day. You've lost weight!"

Bernie, adjusting his glasses following his mother's bear hug, interrupted. "No, Ma, I've <u>gained</u> weight. Listen, listen, you should meet Violet."

His mother stood back, tried to straighten her clothes, and smiled at Violet. "It's so nice to meet you, my dear! I didn't know Bernie had a girlfriend. You are very pretty!"

"Thanks, Mrs. Zellinsky, said Violet. "I've been badgering Bernie to come visit you. You have a nice house," she added, looking around.

The living room was dark with shades and curtains pulled to close out the whistling wind. Big, dark overstuffed chairs were arranged around the room, all facing a small gas grate. A couple of floor lamps with fringed shades stood like sentinels over the chairs On the mantle over the grate were a dozen or more pictures of family members.

"Take off your coats!" continued their effusive hostess, yanking at Bernie's half-unzipped parka. She pointed to chairs and asked, "Would you like some nice chicken soup? I just made it. It'll warm you up!" She started for the kitchen.

"No, no, Ma," Bernie held up his hand. "We're only staying a minute. We gotta get back."

The sound of a squalling baby pierced the room. Down the stairs came a dark-haired woman in her thirties, carrying a tiny, squirming bundle. She stopped at the bottom step as she recognized the visitor.

"Bernie!" she cried. "Where did you come from?" She took the last step and moved quickly over to the pair in the arm-chairs. The baby stopped crying long enough to inspect this newest distraction.

Bernie stood up. "Hi, Rose." They exchanged kisses over the baby's head, as the baby started screaming again. Trying to ignore the noise, Bernie pointed to his companion and said, "This is Violet. Violet, this is my sister Rose."

The women exchanged quick nods and smiles. Violet looked

at the baby and said, "Can I hold him? What's his name? Or is he a her?" She gave a small laugh and held out her hands.

Rose was only too eager to pass over the noisemaker. "It's a he. His name is Moshe, a name his grandfather insisted on, but I just call him Max. I'm sorry about the crying. The doctor says he has colic and that he'll get over it. It can't be too soon for me."

"Hello, Max," cooed Violet, cradling the infant in her arm. Suddenly, the baby stopped crying and stared at the new face looking down at him. For the next few minutes, he sniffed intermittently.

Rose sat on the arm of Bernie's chair. "What brings you to our neck of the woods?" she asked.

"We had an errand at the bank," said Bernie.

"Aha!" said a new voice joining the group from the kitchen. It was Sid, Bernie's oldest brother, who cuffed his younger sibling on the side of the head. "Putting some of your riches away, huh? Something like that had to drag you down here!" he boomed.

"No, we were taking money out," Bernie started to lie, but Violet interrupted him.

"We were renting a safe deposit box," she said, rocking the baby.

"This is Violet," said Bernie quickly.

"Hi, Violet," said Sid. "So, a safe deposit box, huh? You must have a LOT of cash to hide."

"No, just a toy cat," said Violet.

"A toy what?"

"A toy cat," Bernie affirmed. "It's an antique. Belongs to a friend of ours. We're keeping it for him."

"That's a new one on me" said Sid. "What kind of antique cat needs a safe deposit box?"

"Yeah, well, maybe it's not THAT valuable," stumbled Bernie. "But we felt we had to make sure it was safe."

"We were burglarized yesterday," Violet said.

"But they didn't find the cat," Bernie hurriedly interjected.

"Burglarized?" echoed Rose.

"You must be a very attractive target," said Sid. "We knew you were probably doing very well, but I don't think we ever guessed you were doing THAT well!"

"We aren't" said Bernie, suddenly standing up and reaching for his parka. "We just felt we had to protect this kid's antique."

"Soup's on!" called Mrs. Zellinsky from the kitchen.

"Hey, Mom, we gotta go. We just stopped to see how you all were," said Bernie. Violet stood up too and handed the baby back to Rose. The baby started to cry again.

"Listen, Bernie," said Sid, grabbing his younger brother's arm. "If you ever want an appraisal on the cat, I got a friend in the business."

"Yeah, uh, thanks, Sid. I'll keep it in mind." Bernie pulled away, helped Violet with her jacket and backpack, opened the door and blew a kiss to his mother.

And then they were out. Out again in the whiteness and cold.

Violet pulled her hood over her head and looked at Bernie as they made their way carefully down the icy steps.

"What's the rush? I was just getting acquainted!"

Bernie helped her off the last step and stared into the snow.

"Violet, I asked you not to mention the cat."

"You said, 'don't talk about the money.'"

"Same thing. Sid could smell something was up. I just hope he doesn't come looking for us."

They leaned into the wind again, and turned the opposite way from which they'd come. Bernie mumbled something about it being a shorter way back to the bus.

"Why would Sid come looking for us?" Violet asked.

"Because Sid is Sid. He knew we weren't telling him everything."

They turned up another street. Snow was accumulating on parked cars and front stoops. Traffic was creeping by, windshield wipers whap whapping at the driving flakes of whiteness. A figure was running towards them, now in the street, now on the sidewalk.

"Oh crap!" muttered Bernie. "Here comes trouble!"

"What?"

"It's Kicking Bear. I went to school with him."

The figure stopped. A tall man in his twenties. He had on a furry vest, but his arms were bare. A bandanna was wrapped around his head, and a long, scruffy pony tail hung down his back.

"Bernie Zellinsky!" cried Kicking Bear, "What the hell are you doing here??!!"

Bernie wiped a snowflake off his glasses.

"Hello, Bear. We just stopped in to see the family. We're on our way to the bus."

Kicking Bear looked at Violet. "Is this part of your family?"

Bernie pulled his hood up. "This is Violet. She lives with me." Turning to Violet, he said, "This is Kicking Bear. He and I were in school together."

Kicking Bear clarified: "Sometimes together. Sometimes not. Bernie the Wimp and Bear the Delinquent. I coulda been a champ, but I was absent a lot."

Bernie ignored the insult and commented, "Yeah, Bear was a terrific runner...won all kinds of races for our school."

"Until they disqualified me for running in my bare feet," added Bear. "Pure case of discrimination. I'm Native American, you know."

Violet looked at the handsome bronze man. He was kind of grubby, but maybe he'd been at work or something? His jeans were grease-spotted and torn in spots, but incongruously, he had on very nice shoes. Dress shoes. Clotted with snow.

"Well, I kind of guessed, from, you know, your name," she said. "Do you live around here?"

"Yeah," answered Bear. "Right in that house over there, "he pointed. "We're all Native Americans here. This is where they dumped us when they built the park."

"Dumped you?"

"Yeah! The city decided they wanted a park, right where we were living, so they moved us over here and bulldozed all our homes."

"Well, you have to admit, Bear, these are better homes than those you left," interjected Bernie.

"Shit," said Bear. "What do you know, Bernie? How would you like to be ripped out of the place where you'd grown up and shipped out to the edge of nowhere? Yeah, they were junky

72

places, but we were happy there. Upset my grandma so much that she died of a heart attack right after we moved here."

"Sorry, Bear," said Bernie. "I know it must have been tough." He clasped Violet and started to move past Kicking Bear. "Listen, we have to go."

Bear didn't move. "Back to your cozy place in the city, right? Up near the park. Oh yes," he began to ramble, "Up by the rich people. All you honkys and Hebes with your shiksa babes." He glared at Violet. "The city loves you. Ran us Indians off, just like old times when your great grandpappies took over our land and killed us off with smallpox!"

"Sorry, sorry, Bear," Bernie whispered as he pressed past the tall man, hauling Violet along with him. Kicking Bear yelled after them.

"Hey, Bernie! Stop slumming down here! Stay home with your hoity-toity pals. But watch out for us savages. One day, we're going to rise up and you are going to be frigging sorry!"

Bernie and Violet hurried up the slippery sidewalk as the rant continued behind them. Neither said anything for the next block.

Near the bus stop, Violet insisted that they go into a coffee shop, because she was frozen. Sitting over steaming cups, she said, "Did you see his shoes? I wonder where he got them. They looked very expensive, and he certainly wasn't taking good care of them, out there in the snow."

"I'm sorry we ran into him, Vi." Bernie answered. "And sorry about my family. We shouldn't have come over here...should've found another bank to put the cat in."

They zipped up their jackets, adjusted the backpack and went out into the blowing snow. They had to run across the street. The bus was coming.

9

Fernwood pushed through the doors of police headquarters. A cacophony of sound, images and smells attacked his every sense as he moved through the early morning throng. A voice hailed him over the din.

"Hey, Peanut!" It was Betsy Larimer, the big (very big) desk sergeant.

Fern looked up. "Hey, yourself, Juggernut!"

"Naut," corrected Betsy, smiling broadly.

"Nought! Zero!" How true," Fern countered.

Betsy laughed again and guessed at Fernwood's errand. "Looking for Sim? He's here. At his usual stand behind his paper fortress!" She pointed.

Detective Sergeant Simeon Holt sat at a battered desk, almost hidden behind stacks of papers – his "paper fortress" – file folders, old coffee cups and stained paper pizza plates. He was on the phone, pen idly twirling in the fingers of one hand. A half-spent cigar sat smoldering at one corner of the desk, only micro millimeters away from starting a major conflagration.

"Yeah, yeah," he was saying as he waved Fernwood to a chair next to the desk.

"So, what are you waiting for?" continued Sim into the phone as Fernwood cleared the files and notebooks off the chair he'd been offered. "Pick him up. Let's see what he's got. Yeah, yeah. Okay. Talk to you." Sim put down the phone and turned to his visitor.

"Hiya Fern! Why am I honored this morning with your esteemed presence?"

Fernwood ignored the joshing and put an elbow on a pile on the desk.

"I just came down to see how you were doing with that guy they found in the park."

"The lawyer," Simeon confirmed. "Yeah. A really nutty case. I'm up to my ears in it."

"Ah!" said Fernwood. "You could use some help, right?"

"Are you offering?" Sim looked out of the corner of his eye.

"For a fee, of course," smiled Fernwood.

"Listen, Fern," Simeon sat up in his chair. "If you've got something, spill it. If it's worth something, I'm sure there's some finder's funds around someplace. Otherwise, don't use up my day withholding evidence!"

A thin, elderly man came by, carrying a box of coffees in paper cups. Silently, he found a bare spot on Simeon's desk and delivered a cup. "Thanks," mumbled Sim without looking up. Then he looked over at Fernwood. "You want this? I'm already aslosh." He offered the cup to Fernwood, who recognized that this meant he wasn't to be dismissed immediately.

Fern took the lid off the coffee, took a sip and said, "Sim, I think I have something you might be interested in, but I would be more eager to share it if you thought I might be of some ongoing assistance." He took another sip.

"Surprisingly," Sim said, picking up his cigar and puffing it several times. "There is some help I could use, and it might come with all expenses paid."

"The expenses, of course including a fee, yes?" Fernwood sat back in the chair, letting his legs swing.

"Yeah, yeah. Think you might fit us in?" Sim asked almost sarcastically, knowing full well that Fern never turned down a chance at a few bucks.

"Well, what kind of assignment did you have in mind? I have another case I'm working on, but I'm always anxious to help the police..."

"Another case? What are you working on these days, Fern?"

"Oh some funny money found in the park – in fact, not too far from where you found Cabot."

"Money? Near Cabot? Very interesting! Tell me more!"

Oh crap, thought Fernwood. Now he'd done it. The cops are going to be all over this. The dumb cat and the Indian money was complicated enough. He didn't need to have the men in blue mixed in. He tried to brush it off.

"Nothing to do with the Cabot case, Sim. Some kid left a toy in the park. A friend of mine found it and discovered it was full of five dollar bills with the picture of an Indian on them." He squirmed and worked his way back onto the chair, feet dangling. "Sorry I mentioned it."

"What's your connection?" Sim asked.

"Sort of friend of the court. They want to know where the money came from. I'm guessing it came from some sort of Monopoly game, and the kid is afraid to tell his old man."

"Who's his old man?"

Fernwood fidgeted. How the hell had he gotten into this discussion? "Tyler Johnson, the architect. But don't bother him. I see him all the time at the park, and I'll let you know if there's anything interesting."

"I'm already interested," said Sim, writing again in his notepad. "What's the name of the guy who found the cat? I need his address too, if you know it."

"Oh, for crying out loud, Sim! This is just a dopey coincidence. You've got more important things to worry about."

"Listen, Fern..." Sim jammed the cigar into his mouth. It jiggled there as he talked. "Let me decide what's important. You say the cat and the money were near where we found Cabot. I can't just ignore even the remotest possibility that the two things might be related!"

"Please, Sim. Let me handle this," said Fernwood.

"Fern, do you want to help me with this case or not?" Sim stared fiercely at the small man.

Fernwood felt the contract that he had just won... was in danger of slipping out of his hands. He gave the sergeant Bernie's name and approximate address near the park. After writing it down, Sim reached down to a desk drawer and pulled out a laptop computer. Shoving it towards Fernwood, he explained.

"We found this in Cabot's apartment. But we can't break the password. I seem to remember that you're pretty slick at hacking. So I want you see if you can break the code. There could be some very helpful info on the hard drive. If so, there could be some more work for you."

Fernwood stood up. Sim was right, this was right up his alley and who knew what he would find? The computer was a popular Apple model that was supposed to be hard to hack. But he'd gotten into them before. He put on his topcoat and took the computer from the detective.

Sim read his mind. "We think there could be some delicious stuff inside!"

Fernwood cocked his head. "What makes you think that?"

"Well, for one thing..." Sim stood up also... "while Mr. Cabot was not wearing any shoes, it seems he was wearing women's underwear."

—— 10 ——

Detective Sergeant Simeon Holt used the back of his arm to sweep the snow off the unmarked cruiser, because he'd forgotten his gloves. Pulling open the door, he stuffed himself in behind the steering wheel. The car had over 149,000 miles on it, and it smelled of gasoline fumes and stale coffee. Sim switched on the engine. Police cars got hard use, and maintenance was iffy at best. Sim was sure that the whole exhaust system was perforated like a sieve. Someday, he mused, they would find a cop slumped over the wheel, dead from carbon monoxide.

He just hoped it wasn't him. He cracked the side window and pulled out of the lot. Traffic was slow, and white blobs were still falling out of the sky.

He found Bernie Zellinsky's building and pulled into a spot next to a fire hydrant. A man was sweeping snow off the front steps. Sim called to him.

"Mr. Zellinsky?"

The man looked up. "Who's asking?"

"A friend," said Sim walking around the car towards the steps. "Are you Bernie Zellinsky?"

"No. He's in 2A upstairs. You're lucky. I think he's getting ready to go to work. Saw him earlier trying to do his jogging in the park, but the snow's kind of deep and he came right back." The man stepped aside to let Sim go into the building.

Stomping his feet briefly in the vestibule, the sergeant mounted the stairs. Sort of dark. One window at the front afforded minimum light. Sim found the apartment and knocked. After a minute, the door was pulled slightly ajar, a security chain barring further progress. An eye looked out of the opening.

"Yes?"

"Mr. Zellinsky? I'm Sergeant Holt of Municipal Police." He held up his badge so the eye could see it."

"Yes?" repeated the figure behind the door.

"I wonder if you have a minute to answer a couple of questions," Sim answered.

"What kind of questions?"

"Could I come in for a minute? I won't hold you up."

The chain came off the door, and Bernie in underwear stepped back to let the policeman in.

"Pardon me while I keep on dressing," he said. "I gotta go to work."

"I understand," said Sim. "Mr. Zellinsky, we've been told that you found a toy cat in the park a few days ago and that you took it home."

"Who told you that?"

"We're told that you found the cat near a crime scene we were investigating the same morning."

"Oh yeah," said Bernie, pulling on his pants. "But I don't think it has anything to do with your crime scene."

"Well, I wonder if I might see it."

"You could if I still had it, but we were robbed a couple of nights ago, and the cat is gone," Bernie said. The truth was a little warped, but Bernie didn't think the police had to know that he and Violet and stowed the cat in a safe deposit box.

"Robbed?" said Sim. "Was anything else taken?"

"Nope. But whoever it was sure messed up the apartment finding it."

"Were they after the money in the cat?"

"Money?" Bernie feigned surprise.

"We understand the cat was stuffed with money," Sim said evenly.

"Well, yeah," Bernie tried to chuckle. "It was play money. Paper bills with a picture of an Indian on them."

"Did you call the police?"

"No. We didn't think it was warranted. It was just a kid's toy. We were just glad they didn't take anything else."

Sim had pulled out his notebook. "Mr. Zellinsky, I'm curious. What made you pick up the toy? Did you see that it had money in it?"

"No. I didn't find the money till I got it home. No, I picked it up because it looked like somebody had tried to arrange it like a memorial, you know. I was afraid the park people would just throw it away, and I, well, I thought it was kind of sad and deserved better treatment."

"A memorial?" Sim made a note in his book. "What made you think it belonged to a kid?"

"Well, we were talking about finding it when we were up at the Parkview Café the other evening, and some guy came over and said it belonged to his kid – like a remembrance for a pet that had died. We were intending to return the cat to the..."

"Did you know the guy?" interrupted Sim.

"Yeah. It's the architect who designed the park – Johnson, I think. Lives in one of those condos on the edge of the park. Listen, Sergeant, is that all? I gotta hurry or I'll be late for work." Bernie reached for his parka.

"Yes," said Sim, closing his book. "Thanks for your time. We may be back in touch. Meantime, if you think of anything else, here's my card. Give me a call."

Bernie took the card, stuffed it in his pocket and followed the sergeant out of the apartment. Below them, the manager, who had been sweeping the steps, looked up as they started down the stairs.

As they closed the building's front door, a figure approached them, bending against the cold, jacket pulled tightly around her. It was Ruby.

"Hi, Bernie," she called.

"Morning, Ruby." Bernie paused in mid-step. "Off to design another park?" Ruby stopped, breathing clouds of steam.

"Oh yeah," she smiled at the good humored jab. "I'm off to make coffee and file blueprints – my happy lot in life." Bernie caught her brief glance at Holt. He felt that he had to explain him.

"Wait a second, and I'll join you to the bus stop." Turning

towards the big policeman, he said, "This is Sergeant...I forgot your name..." "Holt," Simeon filled in the blank and nodded towards Ruby.

"He's from the police," Bernie went on, now more anxious than ever to resume his walk to the bus stop.

Ruby started to respond, but Holt interrupted. "I think we've met before...Ms..." "Rakovsky," finished Ruby, wondering why the police were visiting Bernie.

"I think you were with my friend Fernwood Grosvenor the other morning when we were investigating that unfortunate incident involving..."

"Jim Cabot," Ruby interrupted. "Fernwood and I jog in the park together. Mr. Cabot's death was kind of a shock to me. He was my father's lawyer."

"Oh?" Sim arched his eyebrows. "Hmmm. You could be of some help to us if you could tell us a little more about Mr. Cabot."

"Could it wait?" asked Ruby nervously. "I'm going to be late for work." She was watching Bernie edging away from the conversation.

"Wouldn't take but a minute," Holt assured her. "I'll give you a lift to your job."

Ruby started to protest when they were interrupted by a voice from down the street.

"Hi Ruby!" It was Fernwood, dressed in a hoodie over his running suit and carrying a paper bag from Starbucks. "I'm glad I caught you. I got us some coffee. Thought we could share a cab downtown." He suddenly caught sight of Simeon Holt.

"Sim! What are you doing in our neck of the woods?"

"Visiting a friend," offered Holt. "Listen, I'm not supposed to use my cruiser like a taxi, but I've asked Ms. Rakovsky to let me take her to work while I asked her about the lawyer we found in the park. I could drop you off on the way."

"Cabot?" asked Fernwood, only too happy to jump in the back of Sim's car. "Why are you asking Ruby about Cabot?"

Holt helped Ruby into the front seat. "She says he was her father's lawyer. I thought she might know something about him that would help us with the case."

Ruby, pretending to be busy adjusting her seatbelt, said "I really don't know much about him. In fact, I thought it was strange that he was in the park at night."

"Why is that?" asked Sim.

"It's not his style. He's not into nature walks, particularly after dark. Or wasn't."

"You seem to know him quite well, Ms Rakovsky," observed Sim.

"He was around the house a lot. He was very friendly towards my sister and me."

"Her sister is Alexandria Vanderhoff," put in Fern, leaning over the seatback.

"Baron Vanderhoff's wife?" Simeon recognized the name of one of the town's leading citizens.

"Yes," said Ruby. "In fact, she probably knows more about him than I do."

"Wait a minute," interjected Fernwood, as the car swerved around a stalled truck. "Cabot isn't the guy you were having an affair with, was he, Ruby?"

"Shut up, Fern." Ruby bristled. "I told you about that in confidence. It has nothing to do with this."

But Holt was curious. "Did you have more than a casual relationship with Mr. Cabot, Ms Rakovsky?"

"Mr. Cabot is – or was – more than 15 years my senior. If you want to know more about him, ask my sister."

They had arrived in front of Ruby's office. She couldn't exit fast enough. Fern tried to give her the coffee he'd brought for her. But Ruby wanted to get away from the two men as quickly as possible. "No thanks!" she practically yelled at Fern and slammed the door.

"Jeez!" said Fern in wonderment. "What did I say?"

"Apparently," said Sim, reaching for the coffee Fern was still offering over the seat, "more than anyone expected." He smiled, flicked the lid off the still steaming liquid and pulled out into traffic.

11

Ruby was sitting on the front stoop of her small apartment. The warm humid day was a surprise interruption to the long winter, and reminded her of the sweet, gentle spring days of her childhood when she sat in the big rocking chair on the shade covered veranda of their old Victorian mansion. As she had rocked along, she had dedicated herself to read every volume of the exciting adventures of Nancy Drew, Amateur Detective.

A familiar voice brought her back to reality. "Someone's been dreaming about something...or maybe it was about someONE!" Violet Simmonds was leaning over the wide cement wall and laughing. "Don't you know it's supposed to be raining any minute now? You'll get drenched out here sitting by yourself!"

"Don't worry about me, Vi," responded Ruby. "I know when to come in out of the rain. Got a minute?" Violet nodded. "Come in for coffee, I need your advice." Ruby opened the heavy door and the two scurried up the steep flight of stairs to the dry, warm comfort of Ruby's apartment.

"I know you like cream and sugar and decaf, Vi. Can I offer you some cheesecake? I made it myself from my mother's recipe. Took me forever. Tricky to get it right."

"I'd be happy and honored, Rube. I'm sure it's delicious."

As she occupied herself starting the coffee and gathering mugs and plates, Ruby struggled to gather words to describe the events that had been troubling her for some time. Before she knew it, the accoutrements had been carefully placed on the table. "You know, Bernie is so happy to be with you, Vi. You've transformed his simple apartment into a perfectly wonderful, homey place. He's very lucky to have met you."

"I'm lucky too," Violet added. "Now tell me what's bothering you."

"It's about Fernwood," Ruby answered. Her hand trembled as she raised the steaming brew to her lips. Before she could take a sip, she stopped to settle herself for a moment. Violet waited quietly to give her time to think.

"Well, it was when we came to tell you about our visit to the archaeologist," Ruby began. "You remember that I confided that I had been an alcoholic. But there's something else. I knew the lawyer who was murdered at the pond. It's something I had kept secret all those years, because..." Ruby covered her face with her hands, trying to stifle burgeoning tears. "I can't go on, Vi. It was so humiliating." Taking her hands away, she looked at Violet, who took them and held them in her own. "Oh, Vi, it was an affair. I had loved him so much and he dumped me. I'm afraid that the police will find out and they will think that I was involved in the murder."

Suddenly, they were startled by a loud knock at the door. Ruby didn't move. Violet was concerned. "You better go and answer it Rube. I'll be here with you."

Ruby got up and slowly inched toward the door. Another rapid knock. Louder this time. She paused, then quickly opened the door.

A tall man in a dripping raincoat towered before her, holding up an official I.D. card. "I remember speaking to you a few weeks ago," he greeted her. Ruby was able to read his name before he swiftly slipped it back into his pocket. "I'm Sergeant Simeon Holt," he continued.

Ruby took a deep breath. "Yes, I remember. Won't you come in? We're having coffee."

Sim shook his head. "Thank you for the invitation, but it would be better for you to come with me. We have some important questions for you." Looking back at Violet, Ruby bit her lip and shrugged her shoulders. Violet was already up to join the pair at the door. Without introducing herself, she crossed between them. "I better be getting back to Bernie," she said. "Call me if I can help. I'll be home all weekend. She dashed into the hall and down the stairs, opened her small umbrella and ducked out into the rain.

Ruby grabbed her hooded windbreaker from the hook on the wall and picked up her purse from the shelf by the door. She accompanied the police officer down the stairs, fearful of what was to lie ahead.

Alexandria Vanderhoff set the controls on the reclining stepper. Seat, number eleven. Arms, number ten. Power, number five. She seated herself and cleared the measures on the face of the equipment. As she began her fifteen-minute routine, her thoughts returned to the events that had precipitated her decision to join the spa at the country club. She recalled the evening she hosted several prominent couples at her new penthouse apartment. She had acquired the apartment after her marriage to the wealthy Baron Von der Hauffe. Aspiring to enter the ranks of the community social register, she had persuaded the Baron to change his family name to Vanderhoff, to appear more socially acceptable to what she considered a new, exclusive and upper class society.

The night of her dinner party, the archaeologist Samuel Collins had engaged Tyler Johnson in a minor tiff at the table. She remembered how it all ended with Collins spilling his water and tipping himself over backward, soaking wet. The unfortunate incident ended with their guests scurrying away in embarrassment. The ensuing altercation with her sister left her sitting alone in the great room, angry and exhausted. The pains in her chest convinced her that she needed to seek physical therapy in the form of exercising at the spa.

"Are you all right, Mrs. Vanderhoff?" Her trainer stood at her side.

"I'm not sure, Charley, maybe you'd better call my husband. I'm not feeling well." Within half an hour, the Baron arrived at the door of the workout room. He hurried to Alexandria where she was resting on a couch along the back wall.

"Good Lord, Alex!" the Baron exclaimed. "Come to your senses. It's about time to call your cardiologist. You can't keep avoiding him like this. You need tests."

~~~~~~~~~~

In the interrogation room, Simeon Holt pulled out a chair from the table, offering it to Ruby. "Miss Rakovsky, I know how inconvenient this is for you. I want to be able to close your file in the case of James Harriman Cabot." Ruby gratefully sat down.

"Your previous connection with him as your family's attorney might give us more information about him - or about others who might give us information concerning the case." He abruptly stopped his habit of pacing while conducting interviews and turned to Ruby. "I will try to make this as brief as possible for you." Pulling a small notebook from his pocket, he sat down across from Ruby.

"Let's begin with Mr. Cabot. First, who were his friends?"

"I haven't the faintest idea."

"Wouldn't you say you knew him well?"

"No."

"Didn't you spend a lot of time with him?"

"Not really."

"Let's discuss Mr. Grosvenor's comment about an affair."

"It was 23 years ago. I was young. He took advantage of me. It lasted three months. That's all."

"Did he have any unusual habits?"

"I wouldn't know."

"All right. Now exactly when was Mr. Cabot first employed as your father's attorney?

"I don't know. Before I was born."

"Were you involved in any of the business Mr. Cabot performed for your father?"

"No. I don't know. Ask Mr. Cabot's partner. He's handling the estate. There are complications."

"What kind?"

"I don't know. Some kind of trust."

"We will need your father's address."

"He died."

"When did he die?"

"A year ago this month."

"Is your mother living?"

"No."

"When did she pass away?"

"Eleven years ago."

"I have your present address. How long have you lived there?"

"I just moved in last year."

"Where did you live prior to the move?"

"With my father."

"Okay. Now can you think back to the day we met – when you appeared with Mr. Grosvenor at the scene where we found the body of Mr. Cabot. Do you remember where you were the day before?"

"Yes, I was home in the apartment."

"Were you alone?"

"No. A friend was with me."

"Who was the friend?"

Ruby decided to tell the truth. "Her name is Violet Simmonds."

"And how long was she there with you?"

"All day."

"What time did she arrive?"

"Twelve o'clock, noon. We had a sandwich."

"And when did she leave?"

"At twelve midnight."

"Miss Rakovsky, can you explain why she stayed so long?"

"It was her day off and she was helping me paint the apartment. When we finished, her roommate picked her up."

"Can you give me the name of her roommate?"

Ruby was getting tired. "Bernie Zellinsky."

"Yes, I have his name. Did you leave the apartment at any time?"

"No. We spent the day painting. It was a big job."

Simeon was pleased. "Just a few more questions and then we'll be through. Referring back to the affair that Mr. Grosvenor mentioned, who else knew about it?"

"No one. Oh, maybe our butler. He caught him dropping me off one night. But he kept it quiet."

"Did anyone else know?"

"Yes. My sister. But I don't think she told anyone. She was angry with me."

"Why?"

"I don't know. Yes, I do. I found out many years later."

"How did you find out?"

"We had a fight."

"What was it about?"

"I don't remember."

"Was she concerned about you?"

"No."

"Why not?"

"Is this really necessary? She just wasn't interested."

Sim suspected that Ruby was holding back. He decided he would have to question the sister and the butler. "So, where does your sister live?"

"At the new condos at the edge of the park."

"Her name?"

"Alexandria Vanderhoff."

"How about the butler?"

"Don't know. Ask my sister. I'm really tired. Do we have to go on?"

"Just long enough for you to sign a statement. I'll have the clerk type it up, and then you're free to go."

Sim closed his notebook and turned to leave. "You can take a chair outside in the waiting room. It won't take long." He held the door for her.

Ruby rose wearily, silent as she passed through the open

door to find an empty chair. She removed the cellphone from her purse and dialed Violet's number. She would need a friend to be with her on her return back to the apartment. The phone was busy.

She noticed a coffeemaker near the reception desk. As she stood up, she caught sight of Fernwood coming in the door. Quickly sitting down again, she turned her back and lowered her head, hoping he hadn't noticed her.

"Hey, Rube," Fern called out as he entered, noting that all the other chairs in the room were empty. Ruby did not respond. He walked over and sat down next to her.

"C'mon, Ruby. Don't be angry."

"How did you know I was here?" she whispered.

"Violet told Bernie, and Bernie told me."

"Fernwood Grosvenor, go away. I don't want to see you."

"Hey, it's late. It took me a long time to get here. Just give me a chance to apologize."

"No way. Leave me alone."

"Hey, I'm really sorry for putting you through this. Just let me see you home."

"Sorry, Fern. I can't forget that you got me into it. I thought you were my friend."

"I am, Rube. Just give me a break. I made a mistake. I want to make it up to you." He stretched out his hand. His voice was trembling. Impulsively, Ruby reached out to him. He clasped her hand and held it for a moment.

"I guess I really don't want to stay angry with you after all," Ruby said softly, lowering her head. "I just felt totally betrayed, and then being harassed by this policeman got me all shaken up."

"Ruby, let's go get the bus. I want you to know that you can trust me from now on."

Sim brought the statement over for her to sign. Then, exhausted, she stood up and allowed Fernwood to lead her to the door. In a way, she was glad it was over.

She was strangely relieved.

And so was Fernwood.

12

In a phone call to Maria about a week after their visit to Loretta, Tyler said, "It is interesting that Loretta mentioned Alexander Rakovsky, Ruby and Alexandria's dad, as a collector of American Indian artifacts. It sparked my curiosity and I've been giving it a lot of thought. If you're up for it, I'd like your reaction to what came to my mind."

"Most certainly," Maria responded.

The two met at the Parkview Café to continue their conversation about their recent visit with Loretta.

"First of all," Tyler said, "is the possibility that Ruby and Alexandria's dad could have been the owner of the certificates."

"And," Maria reacted, "if he was, I think he would recognize their approximate worth. Therefore, it's highly questionable that he would display them with his other artifacts. Do you agree?"

"Exactly! And by the way, I've realized that Jackson and I can't claim ownership, even though it may seem otherwise. We never knew the cat was stuffed like that. So, it seems the next step is to discover and verify the owner."

"If Mr. Rakovsky was indeed the owner," Maria said, "why didn't he put the certificates in a safety deposit box? Anyway, how did they get inside the cat and why?"

"Which brings up my next question," said Tyler. "How many people in the family knew about the certificates? As for the 'why', the only answer I can imagine is to hide them. But what a bizarre situation."

Maria agreed. "Bizarre indeed!"

"I called Bernie and Violet and asked them to meet us here. They should be here soon."

"Didn't your parents say they found the toy cat at the Native American community's annual flea market? Oh! Here come Bernie and Violet now!"

Bernie and Violet breezed into the Café, the wintery chill clinging to their jackets, and saw Maria directing them with a wave. They greeted Maria and Tyler with cheery, expectant smiles, asking how they'd been since their last gathering.

Then Bernie said, "We were anxious to hear about your visit to the Native American community, but first, we want to tell you that after much thought and discussion, Violet and I decided to write a book about our experience being billionaires for a month or two..." He waited for a reaction from their friends.

Maria and Tyler looked at each other, wondering how to reply.

Violet chimed in. "Just kidding," and she and Bernie chuckled.

Bernie continued. "Tyler, we were glad when you called to ask us to meet with the two of you, because Violet and I have been discussing the matter of the certificates. We would like to declare 'finders keepers,' but we have no real connection with any of this. It was only by happenstance that I saw the cat in the park. We can't claim any of it."

Tyler said, "What a coincidence! After some serious thought, I came to the same conclusion, for Jackson and myself."

Violet looked at Bernie and said, "Maybe we should rethink about writing that book. We sure could use some extra money these days...Should we share the news?"

Bernie smiled and said, "Sure, but it's just between the four of us....This fall, we'll be welcoming a little Violet or a little Bernie."

"Ooooh! Congratulations!" Maria and Tyler said in chorus. "That's lovely news," Maria added.

The next few minutes were filled with chatter about the news. Finally, Bernie said, "We've got plenty of time to talk about this. In fact, I can imagine how often you'll be changing the subject when we get together over the coming months." Giving Violet a hug, he added, "So, let's get back on track."

After Tyler and Maria related details of their visit with Loretta and the unfortunate, hateful attack by Kicking Bear, Violet said, "Another coincidence. We too had an unexpected meeting with 'Bear,' and like you, we noticed his shoes..."

Tyler said, "If you were the police sergeant investigating the mysterious death of a prominent man in the park who was shoeless, wouldn't you be curious about Bear wearing such high-style and well-made shoes? It may or may not be a clue, but if I were the police, I sure would want to find out."

Bernie started to say, "And I know just the person..." when Violet elbowed him and with a nod of her head brought his attention to Fernwood Grosvenor, who was about to leave the Café.

Fern had come to the Café to grab a quick lunch and had taken an out-of-the-way booth that allowed him to study some notes about the case he was working on with police Sergeant Sim Holt, hoping to come up with clues he might have missed. He was so absorbed by his work that he never noticed his friends sitting across the room (nor until this moment had they been aware of his presence).

Bernie was out of his chair. He glanced at Tyler and both nodded 'yes' to the unspoken question. Bernie hurried to catch Fern before he opened the door to exit. On the way back to Bernie's table, they both were chuckling as Bernie was telling how he was about to say Fern's name when Violet noticed him and gave Bernie a poke.

Tyler found an empty chair, and everyone shifted to make room for Fern.

As they were telling Fern about seeing the fancy shoes on Bear and of their suspicions concerning them, Maria excused herself saying she saw a friend who had just arrived and wanted to say hello.

Loretta had come to the Café with her friend Clayton Rockford, where they intended to review and consider next steps in their investigation of how some of the original art pieces from Alexander Rakovsky's collection had ended up in the Native American flea market a year ago.

With a big smile and a hug, Maria greeted Loretta, saying "Hi, Loretta! I'm with friends across the room and saw you enter, so I just wanted to say hello and ask how you've been doing since our visit at your place."

Loretta said, "Oh, Maria Dear! Have you met my friend Clayton Rockford?" Clayton stood up and shook hands with Maria as she said, "Not in person, but some of your paintings are like old friends."

Maria explained to Clayton about the visit with Loretta that she and Tyler had made, and their question about what seemed to be antique currency with a picture of an American Indian on it. She then told Maria why they were at the Café.

She continued, "I was surprised to see you, because I come here often, and I had never seen you here before, Loretta. In light of what you just shared with me, I think you would be interested in meeting my friends, and they, I'm sure, will want to meet you. Would you be willing to join us at our table?"

Loretta looked at Clayton, who looking first at Maria, said, "You've stirred my curiosity," and then turning to Loretta, said, "Shall we?"

As Bernie, Violet, Tyler and Fern saw them approaching, there was a scramble to get more chairs and make more space at the table. Introductions were done all around, and Maria said, "Loretta is my very dear friend, and she and Clayton were close friends of Alexander Rakovsky. Just now, they shared with me some information that I believe would be of interest to you. But first, Bernie, would you give a little history of our group, because I believe Loretta and Clayton would be intrigued."

After Bernie shared his, Violet's and Tyler's stories, Clayton said,"Whew!...this...I mean, is anyone keeping notes for a book? This sounds like a mystery bound for the best seller list...almost unbelievable!" Then he turned to Loretta and said, "Loretta, why don't you start by telling about the inventory, and I'll follow with my discovery."

"Yes," began Loretta, "It was before Al Rakovsky's untimely death that he called both of us and asked if we could set up a time to meet, that he had a special reason besides not having seen us for so long. So, we set a date and time, and I invited Al and Clayton to my place. Al's special reason for the meeting was his presentation to both of us of a very artfully rendered inventory of the items in his collection of Native American artifacts, which incidentally included a large number of antique silver certificates with the picture of Chief Running Antelope on them. They are still legal tender and quite valuable. Al explained that he thought we and other artists who had created works in the collection would appreciate knowing where their pieces would be after he died. He said the entire collection is willed to the Museum of the American Indian. We felt honored to receive such a gift from our dear friend.

I would like to add, Tyler and Maria, that they don't call me 'Ancient Woman' for nothing. When you were visiting me recently and asked if I was familiar with such currency, I had forgotten all about the inventory and that the silver certificates were listed there. If I had ever actually seen them, I can't recall."

Then Clayton said, "About two months after Al's death, Loretta and I went to last year's annual flea market. After some time in the hot sun, she joined friends resting in chairs set up in the shade of a cluster of trees, while I continued to mosey among the tables. Suddenly, I began to discover some very familiar pieces, which upon closer examination looked like some I'd seen in Al's collection. With help from a friend, who was one of the market's managers, I was able to collect as many as I could find, so that I could borrow them and check them against the inventory. Indeed there was a match for each piece that we found. So, Loretta and I are here to see how we might proceed with our investigation – beginning with this year's flea market."

Bernie immediately responded. "We have a confession to make, that even some of our friends here don't know yet, but since Loretta and Clayton have shared their reason for being here, it seems the right time to 'let the cat out of the bag,' so to speak. After finding the certificates, we kept them at our apartment for a time, not knowing what to do with them at first, although we knew they were valuable.

"Unfortunately, we were burgled, but oddly, only part of the certificates were taken. We put what was left, including the cat, in a safe deposit box in a bank in a nearby community, which we should have done in the first place, and were still hoping to keep what was left. However, we've since talked it over and realized we couldn't, in good conscience, do that. We are relieved to learn who the legal owner is, and Clayton, if you will provide a way for us to contact you, I will get the certificates and give them to you."

Clayton said, "Thank you, Bernie, but why not leave them in the bank for the time being. I will see if any show up at the flea market, though I doubt any will. I would like to collect as many of the items listed in the inventory as possible and present them to the Museum with a group of the artists who have done some of the work. At Al's request, I've designed a flyer that tells about the collection and which visitors to the exhibit can take with them. In the meantime, I'm going to stop at the police station and tell them about the disappearance of the rest of the collection. Would you like to go with me, Bernie?"

Despite his recent and uncomfortable interview with Sergeant Holt, Bernie said, "Yes, I'd be happy to go with you."

Violet said, "Clayton, Ruby Rakovsky is Al's younger daughter and a friend of mine. If you could get an opportunity to meet and visit with her, perhaps she knows something about her dad's collection that would be helpful in your investigation."

Clayton asked why Violet thought that Ruby might have some idea about the certificates or items found at the flea market.

"I don't know really....just a hunch...She might have something to say which could unwittingly lead you in the right direction."

"Do you have her phone number?"

"Not with me. Sorry."

Tyler jumped in. "I might have it on my phone. She's an employee of my company....yep, here it is."

Ruby was enjoying a Saturday morning after a busy work week, when the phone rang. "Good morning," she said," If this is a sales call, you've got the wrong number."

Oh no, Ms. Ruby, don't hang up. I was a close friend of your dad...My name is Clayton Rockford."

"How did you get my phone number? It's unlisted."

"It's a long story, but I just met some friends of yours, and Dr. Tyler Johnson had your number. I would very much like to meet with you as soon as possible, if you have about an hour somewhere in your schedule."

"Well...I have some time this morning, if you are free."

They agreed on 11 a.m., at her apartment. Ruby called Violet and told her that she had invited a person who said he was a close friend of her dad and that Tyler Johnson had given him her phone number. Violet said she had met Clayton Rockford, but Ruby still felt it was unusual and asked Violet to call her about 11:15, just to make sure everything was okay.

At 11:02, Ruby answered the doorbell, and there stood a very nice looking gentleman who smiled and said, "I'm Clayton..." And Ruby said, "Rockford. Do come in, Mr. Rockford."

"My friends call me Clay, if that's okay with you, Ms. Ruby."

"And you can drop; the 'Ms", if that's okay with you."

Clayton looked around the room and said, "Oh, I see some of my pictures."

"They were gifts from my dad. I never expected to meet the artist." And then the phone rang.

After she answered Violet's call, Ruby said, "Please make yourself comfortable, Clay, and tell me what is so urgent that you wanted to see me."

Clayton told Ruby the whole story of his friendship with her father, the gift of the inventory, about some of the pieces from her father's collection showing up at last year's flea market, and his and Loretta's ongoing investigation.

Ruby was stunned. "My sister and I never paid any attention to Dad's hobby. This is kind of like a mystery novel... But, you know, I think I have a clue." Then she told Clay about her sister's having cleared the house of her dad's possessions, to get it ready for sale, and donating it all to the Indians for their flea market.

Ruby felt comfortable with Clayton from the get-go, and the meeting lasted well past an hour. She accepted Clay's invitation to join him and Loretta when they visited this year's flea market to see if any more of the Rakovsky collection might appear.

Violet arrived home from work a little earlier than usual. She was in an especially happy mood and was starting to make dinner, humming some lullabies she remembered from her childhood, for the little one growing inside her. Soon Bernie arrived. He'd stopped on the way home to pick up a bottle of wine; this time, he'd spent a little more for a better wine than what they normally bought. As he opened the door, he was whistling a happy tune, and when he smelled the wonderful aroma, he called, "Vi! You're home early!"

They both started to talk at the same time, saying "I've got some great news!" then laughing. Bernie kissed Violet and said, "Smells good in here!...Okay, you start. What's your news?" but Vi said "No, it's okay. You tell yours first."

"Well, wanna guess?"

"No, you tell me."

"Well..."

"BERNIE!" Violet commanded.

Bernie took her in a dance position and began to waltz with her, singing "I got a pro-mo-tion to-day with a nice raise in sa-la-ry." And with that he gave her a kiss just as she was about to say "congratulations," as the tears rolled down her cheeks and she hugged him.

Bernie was perplexed. "I thought you'd be happy."

"These are tears of joy," she said, smiling.

"Oh. I didn't know about that kind of tears. Then let's toast the occasion. I bought some really good wine this time. We'll toast the new job and Violetta!"

"Or Bernadito! But Bernie, just a very small amount. It's not good for the baby. Sit down and tell me all about the new job while I serve our dinner."

"Okay, but first, you tell me your good news."

Smiling, Vi said "Well...

"I won't eat while it's hot, unless you tell right now!"

"Oh, alright, if you insist....this is no joke, Bern," and she started to sing, "I got a pro-mo-tion to-day..."

Bernie experienced joyful tears for the first time. "Vi, I am so happy and so relieved. Now we won't have to worry about providing for our child."

"I know, Bernie, I'm relieved too, but we must be thoughtful and plan carefully....Oh Bern! Remember when we first met in the pouring rain? I love you, Bern!"

"Of course. How could you not?"

"BERNIE!"

13

Big, wet blobs of snow were falling all around Fernwood. When the bus pulled up, it splashed dirty slush on his overcoat. Thank God, it was one of those "kneeling" buses that allowed the driver to lower the chassis, to make it easier to enter – a boon for short-legged Fern.

He pushed his way back to a pole he could hold onto with one hand while clutching James Cabot's laptop computer in his other. He had an appointment with Sim Holt down at police headquarters and he was already late. He told himself that he was using the bus because Uber had not been very encouraging about how long he'd have to wait for a ride. In truth, he was maxed out on his credit cards, and he hoped Holt would give him an advance on his contract to hack Cabot's encrypted computer.

When the bus stopped again, he let go of the pole and tried to brush some of the slop off his coat. This and his delay in getting downtown were beginning to make him tense.

When he put his hand back on the pole, it inadvertently touched the hand of another passenger. Fern looked up. It was a tall, somewhat chubby boy, maybe fourteen or fifteen. Fern mumbled an apology and moved his hand. The boy stared down at him.

"Are you a man?" the boy asked abruptly.

"I beg your pardon?" Fern said.

"You're really short," said the boy. "I'll bet my kid brother is taller than you."

"Well, that's his problem," retorted Fern, not really wishing to continue this conversation.

"It ain't a problem," said the boy. "He could probably beat you up."

"Why would he want to do that?" Fern was beginning to get irritated.

"Because you're a midget."

A large man bundled in a hooded jacket and sharing the pole with Fern and the boy, suddenly interjected. "Hey, kid, leave him alone."

"Fuggoff, Mister" the boy turned towards the man. "You ain't my father."

Fernwood was about to suggest that everybody let the discussion drop, when the bus arrived at his stop. The rear door opened, and he shoved his way to the exit.

"Have a good day, Everybody!" he smiled through gritted teeth at the boy. But the boy was busy returning the stare of the interloper who wasn't his father.

Boy, what a crappy day, Fern thought as he made his way up the block to police headquarters. The wet, noisy crowd in the day room didn't make him any happier, especially when it was a few minutes before Sergeant Simeon Holt returned to his desk.

"Sorry, Fern. I was in the head. Whaddya got?"

Fernwood took off his coat, carefully hung it on the back of the chair, and plunked the laptop on Sim's cluttered desk. Patting the computer, he said, "Well, after a lot of effort, I broke the code and found some very interesting stuff."

"Like what?"

"Well, for one thing, I found inventories of a lot of Cabot's clients' estates."

"Yeah? So?"

"...including that of Mr. Alexander Rakovsky, the rich daddy of my friend Ruby and her sister Alexandria Vanderhoff."

"And...?"

"Well, among all the stocks and bonds and stuff, I found that Mr. Rakovsky collected Native American artifacts, and among these things he had a collection of 100-year-old U.S. currency with a picture of an Indian Chief on it."

"Well. La-de-dah," said Holt, leaning back in his swivel chair and relighting his cigar.

"This could be significant, Sim," Fern insisted. "Remember I told you about the toy cat that Bernie Zellinsky found in the park? Near the murder scene? It was stuffed with money that looks like the currency described in Rakovsky's estate."

"Zellinsky said it was stolen from him."

"Oh yeah? I didn't know that."

Holt sat forward in his chair. "Which causes me to ask you

how you know what his money looks like."

"Bernie gave me a sample to check out with a friend at the city museum. It's very valuable, and Bernie had a lot of it."

"So you think Cabot somehow got hold of it and got clonked while burying it in the park?"

"No." Fernwood slid off the chair where he'd been sitting, put his hands behind his back and looked down at the floor, pondering. "I'm not sure what I think. Tyler Johnson's kid planted the toy cat in the park, but Johnson didn't know it had money in it."

"Where did the kid get the cat?"

"Johnson said his parents found it at a flea market uptown where a bunch of Indians live."

"Sounds like coincidence to me."

Fernwood got back up on the chair. "Except that the notes on Rakovsky's estate indicate that both Cabot and Rakovsky were into a lot of charity for the Indians."

"Boy, that's a stretch, Fern. Wish those two guys weren't dead so we could interview them."

"Well, maybe we – that is, you – could talk to the daughters. I don't want to say anything to Ruby. I'm already in deep doodoo with her for telling you about her connection to Cabot."

"Sounds like Ruby would be more help to us than her sister."

"I'm not sure. Take a look at this." Fernwood opened the laptop, punched a few keys, and showed Holt the screen. "This is an email between Alexandria and Cabot. Pretty hot stuff. Nothing about Daddy's estate but a lot about an affair between the two."

"I thought you said that Ruby was the one who was having the affair."

"That was a long time ago. This is recent. Just a few months ago. And this isn't the only email. There's a wad of juicy messages between Mrs. Vanderhoff and Cabot.

"Haw!" Sim suddenly exploded. "Maybe that's where the underwear came from!" He reached into a desk drawer and pulled out a Ziploc bag containing a pair of folded women's panties. "I got these from the Evidence Room. These were what the dignified Mr. Cabot was wearing when we found him."

Fernwood looked at the garment. "Man, it looks like very expensive underwear. I thought maybe Cabot was into something funny – psychological – you know, like a fixation on his mother or something."

"I'm having them analyzed, to see if we can find out where he got them," Sim said. "All we have so far is embroidered initials on them — A. R. V."

"Not the initials of James Harriman Cabot," Fern observed. He stopped. "I just had a creepy thought: A. R. V. Alexandria Rakovsky Vanderhoff."

Sim couldn't help himself. He started to laugh. "Cabot was wearing his girlfriend's panties?? Boy! That's pretty perverse!"

Fern smiled too. "You never know where true love will lead you."

Sim pulled out his notebook and penciled in a message to himself. "Well, looks like I should invite Mrs. Vanderhoff down here and ask her if she's missing any of her delicate wear."

—— 14 ——

Swirling snow. Another late winter flurry. Ruby Rakovsky closed the door, pulled her hood over her head and hurried to the bus stop. It was Monday and the beginning of another week of work at Tyler Johnson's architectural firm.

At the bus stop she was surprised and pleased to find her friends Bernie and Violet waiting to go to work too. When the bus finally came, splish-splashing up to the curb, the trio piled in and found seats near each other.

"I'm so tired of this winter!" said Violet. "I wish it would suddenly stop and be replaced by a nice 65-degree day with birds chirping..."

Ruby chuckled. "You and me both! Especially tonight. I have to go to a reading of my father's will."

"Oh, that should be interesting," said Bernie, who had stood to give an elderly woman his seat and was now holding onto a stanchion and leaning over his two friends.

"'Interesting' may be one word," said Ruby. "But I'm not looking forward to it. My dear sister will be there, and I have an uncomfortable feeling that all will not go smoothly."

One by one, the three departed the bus, scurrying across wet sidewalks into their respective workplaces. The day began warming up and the snow stopped.

At about 10:00 a.m. Sim Holt ushered Ruby's sister Alexandria into the interrogation room at police headquarters. She'd come at his invitation, accompanied by her husband, Baron Walter Vanderhoff. Sim had asked the Baron to wait in the outer lobby while he interviewed Alexandria alone.

"Why didn't you let my husband accompany me??" demanded Alex before plopping down in the seat offered by Holt.

"Well, you may find some of my questions –uh – delicate," Sim said, taking the other chair in the room. "If you decide later that you still want him here, I'll bring him in."

"What do you mean, 'delicate'?" Alex asked.

"Let's start at the beginning," said Sim, arranging papers in front of him. "First, Mrs. Vanderhoff, thank you for coming down this morning…"

"What a gross hour for a meeting!" Alex interrupted. "Do you realize what time I had to get up in order to be here by ten???"

"Yes, and I thank you again for being prompt," Sim said. "Now, Mrs. Vanderhoff, let's get right to the point. Do you know James Harrison Cabot?"

"You mean the man they found murdered in the park? Yes! He was my father's lawyer."

Sim cleared his throat. "I meant, were you more intimately acquainted with Mr. Cabot – beyond your father's professional relationship?"

"How do you mean?" Alex sat up. "He was often a guest at the house. We had dinner with him many times."

"But apart from that, did you have a personal, individual relationship with Mr. Cabot?"

"That's a strange question!" rejoined Alex. "He's (or was) decades older than I!"

"The reason I ask, Mrs. Vanderhoff, is that we found that Mr. Cabot was wearing this garment, when we discovered him in the park," said Sim, pulling out embroidered panties from the folder in front of him. "They are definitely feminine underwear, and they have the initials A R V embroidered on them."

"So?" said Alex, leaning back in her chair and folding her arms. "There must be thousands of women with those initials – and why would Cabot be wearing feminine panties?"

"Well, that was exactly my question," said Sim, fingering the underpants. "But it just seemed highly coincidental that Mr. Cabot was intimately acquainted with your family, that he was found near your home and that he was wearing clothing with your initials...."

Alexandria began to cry. She grabbed the panties Sim was holding and pulled them to her chest.

"Okay, okay!" she sniffed. "They're mine! Only, God knows why he was wearing them! He left his own shorts behind!"

"Left them behind? Where?" Sim started to put his hand on hers, thought better of it, and withdrew it.

"In our bedroom! Walter found them! Under the bed. And he knew immediately that they weren't his! Oh, God, this is terrible! He knew, and I couldn't do anything but confess and ask his mercy!" Alex was now sobbing. "And I still can't believe it, but the next night, he brought me roses and told me he forgave me!!!"

Sim fished around for a handkerchief, but Alex had already found one in her purse.

"So," said Sim quietly, "you're telling me that on the night of his murder, Cabot was in your bedroom with you?"

"Yes, and then, and then...we heard Walter come in downstairs. He was early! Really early! And, oh God, I didn't know what to do! And Jim, Mr. Cabot, was jumping into his clothes, and I don't know, he must have put on my underwear by mistake..."

"And did your husband find the two of you together?"

"No, no," sniffed Alex, "There's a back stairway down to the kitchen, and Jim went out that way – so it was awhile before Walter knew what was going on."

"When you say 'awhile,' about how long before your husband realized there was an intruder in the house?"

Alex tried to compose herself. "Oh, not until the next morning. The night before, he'd come into the bedroom and saw the bed was a mess – but he thought I was having another one of my attacks. I have heart problems..."

"So he didn't hear Mr. Cabot's departure down the back stairs?"

"No. Jim was very quiet. I'm not even sure he put on his shoes. He just snuck out of there. Really silent. Walter didn't suspect anything. Until he found the undershorts the next day."

"Hmmm," mused the sergeant. Suddenly, he scraped back his chair and stood up. "Mrs. Vanderhoff, thank you again for coming in. I think, if you don't mind, I'll ask you to sit out in the waiting room while I ask your husband a couple of questions."

"You don't think Walter did anything, do you?" Alex was alarmed. "I told you he didn't even know Jim was in the house until I told him the next day. He was angry, but before he could do anything about it, they found Jim in the park..."

"Thank you again," murmured Holt, helping Alex out of her chair, out through the noisy office and out into the waiting room.

The Baron started to help Alex on with her coat when Sim asked if he would join him for a moment.

"Just me?" asked the Baron. "Or would you like both of us?"

"Just you for now," said Holt, indicating the way back through the office. Turning to Alex, he said, "We'll only be a few minutes."

In the interview room, the Baron laid his damp coat on the table and placed his hat on top of it. Nodding in Sim's direction, he took a chair as Holt let himself down in the other.

"I have just a few questions," began Holt. "I understand you know James Cabot."

"The man found in the park?" said the Baron. "Only slightly. He was the lawyer for my wife's father. I met him once or twice at dinners at the Rakovsky home."

"I won't beat around the bush," continued Sim. "Your wife said you were aware that she and Mr. Cabot were having an affair."

The Baron shifted in his chair, stared for a moment at the detective, coughed and said, "So she informed me."

Sim waited a minute for the Baron to continue. When he didn't, Sim pressed on. "More specifically, Mr. Vanderhoff, she indicated that you came upon them in bed together at your home on the night that Mr. Cabot was found in the park."

The Baron harummphed. He then sat forward and put his clasped hands on the table.

"That's not quite true, and I'm not sure why you are bringing up this upsetting and private part of our lives."

"Oh, I think you see quite clearly," said Sim. "I am wondering if you pursued Mr. Cabot as he tried to escape from the house..."

"Pursue him??! I didn't even know he was in the house until my wife told me the next morning. Look here, Sergeant, I don't know what you're implying, but you are not only insulting, you're wasting my wife's and my time!" The Baron started to reach for his coat.

"I'm only trying to get at the facts," said Sim evenly. "A man comes home, finds his wife in bed with another man, and the next morning that other man is found dead from a blow to the head in the nearby park."

"I didn't find *anybody* in bed with my wife!" The Baron stood up, now red in the face.

"And" continued Sim, also standing, "he chases the man out of his house and into the park, where in his anger he strikes and accidentally kills him..."

The Baron grabbed his coat, slammed his hat on his head and started moving towards the door. "I didn't chase anybody! I think you people are desperate to find a culprit, and I truly resent your trying to implicate my wife and me. If we're through here, I'm leaving to take my wife home and call my lawyer!"

Sim reached the door first, turned around and faced the Baron.

"Mr. Vanderhoff, we are merely doing our job. If indeed, you never saw Mr. Cabot in your bedroom and never left the house, you have nothing to worry about."

"My wife will swear to it!" the Baron practically shouted. And reaching past Sim, he opened the door, marched briskly through the office and into the waiting room. Sim followed him and put a gentle hand on the fuming Baron's elbow as the latter was reaching for his wife's coat.

"Thank you both again for coming down," said Sim, trying to avoid a tone of sarcasm. "Please don't leave the city until we can clear this up."

But the Vanderhoffs were already exiting into the bright sunshine. Sim watched as they hailed a cab and drove off.

At home, the Baron hung up their coats and found a chair in the parlor for Alexandria, who was still breathing heavily and patting her chest.

"Just sit quietly, my Dear, and I'll have Quinn bring us some tea," referring to the butler. But when he entered the kitchen, the cook told him that Quinn had gone off on a personal errand. Still boiling, the Baron allowed the cook to steer him back into the parlor with assurances that tea would be forthcoming immediately.

"Put some brandy in mine," said the Baron.

That evening, the Vanderhoffs welcomed Harvey Palmhizer, attorney and former assistant to James Harriman Cabot. He was joined minutes later by Alexandria's sister Ruby who was accompanied by Fernwood Grosvenor. The Baron had never met Fernwood before and he couldn't help staring at the very short man. Fernwood smiled and extended his stubby hand. The Baron hesitated and then limply shook the hand.

Moments later, the company was seated and the Baron was offering drinks. Ruby and Alexandria had chosen seats as far from each other as possible.

When introductions were complete, the lawyer opened his briefcase and pulled out manila folders. "I think everybody knows that we are gathered here tonight to hear the last will and testament of Alexander P. Rakovsky."

When his audience sat silently and expectantly, Palmhizer opened the document and began to read. The language was traditional with assurances that the testator was "of sound mind". The bulk of his estate, consisting of various investments, he split evenly between his two daughters, "except for my collection of Native American crafts and ephemera."

The lawyer paused at this point and pulled out a second document. He explained that this was an inventory of the Native American collection and offered to read it. Ruby and Alexandria demurred, saying they could save reading until afterwards. Palmhizer returned to the will and read the stipulation that the collection should be given to the "Museum of the American Indian," listing the address and contacts.

Alexandria sighed aloud. "Oh God, I think I gave all that stuff to the local Indians." She took a breath and added, "Same difference, though. Indians are Indians. I don't think Daddy would argue."

But Ruby objected. "There IS a difference, Alex! When I saw those people from the Indian neighborhood loading the truck from the house, I TOLD you that you should have had at least the decency to consult with me..."

"And what would that have gained?" sniffed Alexandria. "Did you want any of that stuff? I did us both a favor by getting rid of it, so we could sell the house. Along with all of Daddy's worthless antiques, it was just a lot of crockery which nobody was interested in!"

"There were a lot of valuable things!" countered Ruby, "and you had no right to dispose of them before the will was read!"

"Valuable??" chuckled Alexandria. "It was just Daddy's junk collection! What makes you think it was valuable?"

"For your information, Alex, I was visited recently by an artist who was a good friend of Daddy's and who discovered a lot of his collection at a flea market the Indians had last year. Daddy told him that he had intended to give those things to the museum, and Clayton was going around the market trying frantically to keep any more of it from being sold!"

"Hah!" snorted Alexandria, "I'll bet a penny on the dollar that the Indians probably got more for that junk than the museum would ever realize."

"You don't know anything, Alex! One thing that was sold was a bunch of antique money worth thousands! But nobody knew it because it was stuffed inside a toy cat!"

"Oh, now I've heard everything," scoffed Alexandria. "Antique money? Stuffed inside a toy? Why would Daddy have anything like that??"

"Ladies, please, may I interrupt?" interjected Lawyer Palmhizer. "Let's read the rest of the will and then you can deal with the question of the collection."

With grumbling and biting of lips, the sisters each sat back in their chairs, silently glaring at each other. The lawyer picked up the will again and read that "in view of the fact that my older daughter Alexandria is apparently happily married and ensconced in a fine home, I leave my land and home and all its contents except the collection afore mentioned, to my younger daughter Ruby."

"What??" Alexandria sat upright. "That's crazy! What does Ruby want with that house?? That big mausoleum?? Surely Daddy meant..."

"No, that's the specific instruction in the will," said the lawyer.

Ruby sat stone faced.

Later, after Palmhizer had passed out copies of all the documents, the visitors filed out of the house. On the way home, walking in the crisp air beside Fernwood, Ruby mused.

"You know, Alex is right. What do I want with that big old house? We had a maid and a butler to take care of it, and it was always in need of some repairs...I don't need that kind of responsibility, and I certainly don't need all that space to bounce around in!"

Fern put his arm around her. "Ruby, that was a very difficult session tonight. I don't know what got into your sister. If she'd been a man, I think I would have gotten up and busted her in the mouth!"

"Oh, Fern!" said Ruby, sniffing and chuckling at the same time. "Alex has always been that way. I don't know why I let her stir me up like that – but I just couldn't let her wiggle out of blame for that big mistake she made with the collection and furniture and all that."

Then Ruby stopped abruptly.

"But you know, Fern, I somehow can't just sell the house. It has so many memories. It was where I grew up. I..."

"Well. You could always rent it..."

"Who would rent an enormous place like that?"

"You never know. But hey, you could divide it up into apartments, rent it out to students or artists, or maybe even some of the Indians..."

Ruby had to think about that.

Meanwhile, Alexandria was also thinking. Stewing. Pouting. Her husband tried to interest her in another drink, but she waved him away.

"Walter, I have never had a night like this! The nerve of my sister, talking to me like that! And that stupid will...Ruby must have written it for Daddy. Giving her the house! You would have thought he would have at least divvied owner-ship between us, 50-50!"

She clutched at her chest.

Baron Vanderhoff tried to comfort his wife.

"You had a very strenuous day, Dear," he said, patting her hand.

"You're not kidding!" Alex shifted in her chair, rubbing her chest and shoulder. "Talking to that policeman this morning! What right did he have nosing into our private affairs!!??" She clutched at her chest again. "Now, it's going to be all over town! What will our friends say??!! Oh, Walter! Call the ambulance!"

An hour later, Alexandria was in the ICU in the city's main hospital. Her husband sat in the waiting room, alternately taking off, and putting on, his hat.

"Your wife has had a quite severe heart attack," said the doctor. "We're trying to stabilize her now."

"Is she going to be all right?" asked the Baron.

"We'll know in the next few hours," said the doctor.

Two days later, Alexandria woke in a private room in the hospital. Her husband, who had been sitting vigil, was gone. Instead, her sister Ruby sat in the visitor chair.

"Hello, Alex," said Ruby softly.

Alexandria took a moment to adjust to the morning sunlight and the figure across the room.

"Ruby!" she wheezed, "What are you doing here?"

"I came to see my sick sister," said Ruby.

"Oh, God," said Alexandria. "You can't imagine what I've been through!"

"You've had a pretty rough patch," agreed Ruby.

"I don't know why you came...After all the mean things I said to you, Ruby. Oh, I am such a mess. No wonder God took a swipe at my heart!"

"I don't think God was paying any attention to our squabbles, Alex. Things just happen. I'm so sorry they happened to you. But I'm glad that you're on the mend!"

"I can't believe those words coming out of the mouth of my little sister!" Alex tried to sit up and reach for a glass of water. Ruby got up and helped her take a sip. Alex rambled on.

"I've been such a wretch all my life! Jealous of my sweet little sister! So good. So pretty. So smart. No wonder you were Daddy's favorite!"

"That's not true, Alex," said Ruby softly. "Daddy loved us both. I think it was just hard being the oldest child. More was expected of you..."

"Ruby, I've been mean to you all of our lives. I've been lying here thinking about it. Why am I so mean? I have everything any sane person could want, a wonderful, loving husband, a grand home, the means to own or do anything I want...And most of all, I have a dear sister who has stuck by me through thick and thin, through all the insults, and all the..."

"Alex," interrupted Ruby, "Relax. You're a sick woman and you're agitating yourself unnecessarily. Lie back. Enjoy the sun. Let people love you. There's a lot of life ahead of you.

Get better fast so you can enjoy it."

~~~~~~~~~~~~~~~~

It was Saturday, and the bank in Bernie Zellinsky's old neighborhood was closing at noon. Bernie and Violet waited while the clerk found their safe deposit box and brought it to the cubicle where they sat. When the clerk left them alone, Bernie pulled the toy cat out of the box. Checking to make sure the rolls of silver certificates were still inside, he started to stuff it into Violet's shopping bag and then paused.

Staring at the toy's impassive face he said, "Well, I guess this is the end of a very strange story. Who would've believed it – and who would have believed that we're giving up all this money??"

Violet held the bag while he put the cat inside.

"Hey, Bernie, it's the right thing to do. We could never have lived with ourselves if we'd kept it. The sooner we turn it over to Clayton the better. The museum is the right place for it."

"Yeah," agreed Bernie as they stepped out onto the street. "I called Clayton, and he's meeting me at the café this afternoon to pick it up."

Violet put her hand on Bernie's arm. "Wait. Let's not go home through your old neighborhood. Much as I'd like to see more of your family, I don't want to run into that Kicking Bear guy again. He really scared me."

"Okay, but I wouldn't worry. Fernwood said he told the cops about Bear's shoes, and they're going to talk to him." After they had walked a few minutes, Bernie added, "Kicking Bear is one crazy guy, but I don't think he'd kill somebody for their shoes."

That afternoon, the temperature had risen into the fifties, and the Parkview Café was crowded. Bernie and Violet soon found Clayton, Ruby and Fernwood at a table, pulled up chairs and joined them.

"Well, here it is," said Bernie, plunking the shopping bag with its precious cargo on the table.

"Thanks, Guys," said Clayton, taking the bag and stuffing it between his knees. "I'll take good care of it and make sure it gets to the museum... Meantime, let's order drinks and toast the beginning of a successful ending!"

As they sat sipping their drinks, Fernwood said "I told Holt about Kicking Bear's shoes, and he's going to talk to him. That would sure be a weird turn if Bear is involved in the lawyer's death." Shifting forward in his chair, so his toes could reach the floor, he went on.

"Speaking of lawyers, Ruby and I went to the reading of her father's will the other night."

"Oh?" said Bernie, "How did that go?"

"Very well," said Fernwood, smiling at Ruby and taking a gulp of his drink. When Ruby frowned at him, he put his hand over his mouth. "Oops, sorry Ruby! It's your private business..."

Ruby waved her hand. "That's okay, Fern. It was an interesting night, and that's an understatement. My sister had a heart attack."

"Oh my God!" Violet burst out. "What happened?"

"After she went home, it hit her, and her husband had to call an ambulance. She was in the ICU, but she's in a private room now and I think she's going to be okay."

"Did the will upset her?" asked Bernie.

"Well, I'm sure some of the details added to her stress. She'd been interviewed by the police that morning – about our dad's lawyer being found in the park."

"Yeah," interjected Fernwood, "I think the will did upset her. She made a big mistake when she gave away Rakovsky's Indian collection. It wasn't hers to give. The old man left the house and contents to Ruby and willed the Indian stuff to a museum."

"Ruby owns the house 100%?" Bernie asked. I'm glad for you, Ruby, but I can understand why your sister might be upset."

"Oh, Alexandria didn't suffer," put in Fernwood. "The old man had plenty of money and he split it between the girls, right Ruby?"

"Still, I'm sure it hurt Alexandria when she found out she didn't share in the house where she grew up," said Ruby. "As it is, I don't know what I'm going to do with the place. It's enormous. Too big for me. I'm thinking of selling it, which will probably upset Alex all over again."

"I told Ruby she should divide it up into apartments and rent it out," said Fernwood.

"Actually, it's located near a high-rent commercial district," observed Violet. "You could probably turn it into offices or stores or something."

Ruby was about to protest that she wasn't enthusiastic about being a developer, but Fernwood chimed in again.

"Hey Rube! Don't blow off the idea too quickly. Talk to your boss, Tyler the architect. I'll bet he knows some contractors who could give you a rough idea of what's involved."

The group chattered on about the possibilities, ordered another round of drinks, and as evening began to settle on the park, decided to have supper together.

15

On the fourth floor of the city's tallest building is a currency exchange shop called International Money Exchange. The proprietor is Eric Swenson, the third generation to manage the business his grandfather started when he first moved to America from Sweden. Like his father and grandfather before him, Eric has always been fascinated by the endless variety and the romantic histories of monetary media. As the name of his business implies, he does business around the world, with individual collectors and a spectrum of financial institutions.

There's not much foot traffic at the Exchange. Eric does most of his business via the Internet, so he was momentarily surprised when a man in a fitted overcoat and an old fashioned fedora walked in. The visitor took a brief look around the walls of the shop with their displays of coins and currency, and then walked up to the counter.

"Good morning!" Eric greeted the man. "How can I help you?"

The man spoke with a trace of a British accent.

"I have some antique currency," he said, "and I'd like to know how much it's worth." Unbuttoning his overcoat, he pulled a paper bill out of his suit pocket and laid it on the counter. Eric picked it up and smiled.

"A Running Antelope!" he identified the bill. "I haven't seen one of these in a long time! Wherever did you find it?"

The customer seemed to hesitate. "Uh – my sister inherited a collection..."

"A collection? If this is what I think it is, it's quite valuable. Do you have more?"

"I have several rolls of it. When you say 'valuable', how much is it worth?"

"Well, Mr. – ah..."

"Quinn," filled in the customer.

"Well, Mr. Quinn, this is a very limited edition of a five-dollar certificate that the government printed over a hundred years ago. I'm frankly quite excited to see it – in fact, so much so that I'd like to have a collector friend of mine take a look at it. I think he would be especially interested. Do you have a few minutes? He's nearby and I'll bet he'd come right over to examine it. If it's what I think it is, he'd probably be willing to pay a good price for whatever you have!"

Mr. Quinn was obviously quite pleased. He paused for only a moment before agreeing to wait for Eric's friend to come and look at the certificate.

Eric made a phone call, punctuated by an enthusiastic description of the money, and twenty minutes later, a large man in a parka came in the door, blowing on his hands.

"Hi, Eric," boomed the man. "Whaddya got?"

"Hi, Sim!" Eric greeted the new arrival. "I'm sorry to interrupt you, but I thought you'd like a first chance to look at what Mr. Quinn here has brought in." He pushed the bill across the counter towards Sim.

Sim took the certificate and leaned over the counter to give the money better light. After squinting at it a minute, he looked up, first at Eric and then at Quinn.

"Well, Mr. Quinn, Eric is right. This is something special. Where did you get it, if I may ask?"

Quinn repeated his story about his sister's inheritance.

"Do you live with your sister?" Sim asked. "Just curious."

"No, I live by myself. I'm butler to Baron Walter Vanderhoff – you may have heard of him?"

"Oh, yes," Sim nodded. "I think everyone in town knows the Baron. He's married to one of Alexander Rakovsky's daughters, isn't he?"

"Yes," answered Quinn. "As a matter of fact, I was butler to Mr. Rakovsky before he passed away. His daughter Alexandria kindly hired me for their household after his death."

"Rakovsky, huh? Big philanthropist, right? I think he gave his collection of Indian stuff to the American Indian Museum – or at least I heard that was his intention."

"It's quite possible," muttered Quinn.

"Mr. Quinn, I didn't introduce myself. I'm Sergeant Detective Simeon Holt of the city police department. I happen to be privy to a list of items in Mr. Rakovsky's Indian collection. My particular interest in your certificate is that a bunch of them were in the collection but have mysteriously turned up in a toy cat found in the city park."

"Oh?" Quinn put on an expression of mild curiosity. "I thought you were a collector." He looked at Eric.

"I am a collector of information. We traced the cat and the money to the man who found it, but when we interviewed him, he claimed that it had been stolen from him. He had been burgled."

"Not all of it," blurted Quinn.

"What?"

"I meant that I am surprised that all of it was taken."

"Why?"

"Well, I – uh – seem to remember that Mr. Rakovsky did used to show it to visitors but he didn't seem to put much value on it."

"What makes you say that?"

"Well, he treated it rather casually. I mean, he would leave rolls of it lying on his desk in plain view. Personally, I would have put it in a safe or something."

"Why? Did you think it was valuable?"

Quinn nervously buttoned up his overcoat.

"They were worth at least five dollars apiece, and they had that picture of an Indian on them, which I thought would add to their value."

"So you squirreled them away for safe keeping?" Sim watched Quinn's hands still fussing with his overcoat buttons.

Quinn suddenly stopped twitching and put his hands in his pockets.

"I confess that I was worried about them during the chaos in the house immediately after Mr. Rakovsky died...

"Like, somebody could have just picked them up and walked off with them?" Sim offered.

"Exactly. So I took it upon myself to hide them until a safe disposition was decided upon."

"Where did you hide them?"

"Where I thought nobody would think to look. I stuffed them into one of the toys that the children played with when they were young. It had been more or less abandoned in the attic."

"A toy cat?"

"Yes. But later when I went to retrieve it I discovered it had been taken away with the rest of Mr. Rakovsky's collection when Miss Alexandria donated everything to the Indian community."

"But not before you helped yourself to some samples..."

"Just this single sample which Mr. Rakovsky gave me."

"Mr. Swenson here told me that you told him you had 'several rolls' of the certificates."

Quinn took his hands out of his pockets and began fiddling with his buttons gain. He looked helplessly at Eric.

"I had hoped he had forgotten that," he chuckled lamely.

"Those rolls didn't really come from your sister, did they?"

"No. As I say, they were gifts from Mr. Rakovsky."

"Or were they stolen from Bernie Zellinsky?"

Quinn choked.

"Not stolen. Retrieved. They didn't belong to Zellinsky."

"How did you know he had them?"

"I overheard a conversation at a party at the Baron's house where I was serving dinner."

Sim had unzipped his parka and was now leaning on the counter, still fingering the note.

"So, you went to Zellinsky and asked him to give you the money?"

Quinn undid his overcoat.

"Well, Mr. Zellinsky wasn't at home…"

"So, you just helped yourself?"

"Of course. The money wasn't his, and I felt that at least part of it was mine…"

"Because Mr. Rakovsky had given it to you?"

"Not specifically. I felt I was owed some extra compensation for my long service to the family, and I was not certain I would be part of Rakovsky's will."

"So you gave yourself sort of a tip?"

"Sergeant, you have to realize that these people were filthy rich, and while they provided me with a job, they were not particularly generous in their remuneration. I thought that the bills would kind of even things up, and they would never be missed…"

"Mr. Quinn, you've committed outright theft, twice over."

Quinn felt faint, and reached for the counter to steady himself.

"I didn't take all of it. I left a lot of it in the cat."

"Oh really?" Sim raised his eyebrows. "Why was that?"

"I could see that Mr. Zellinsky lived in modest circumstance, as I do. There were a number of rolls in the cat. I thought that if the currency was worth anything, it behooved me to share, even though I had an important need for the money."

"Yeah," agreed Sim, who reached out to catch Quinn, who was now beginning to sag. "We all have an important need for money."

"No, no," rasped Quinn, "you must understand – my sister..."

"Hey, Quinn," interrupted Sim, "leave your sister and her phony inheritance out of this. I'm wondering if you even have a sister."

"She lives alone, like I do. She has stage 4 cancer, and she's destitute. I have no savings, but the certificates here might provide some help with her medical bills..."

Sim helped Quinn stand up straight.

"Mr. Quinn, if what you're saying is true, I'm sympathetic. But her needs don't justify stealing. My car is outside. Please give me the rest of the rolls, and let's go down to the station to complete this interview."

Quinn, still a little unsteady, reached in his pocket and pulled out several rolls of the currency. Handing them over to the sergeant, he asked, "Are you arresting me?"

"Not yet," said Sim, grasping Quinn gently by the arm. "First, I have more questions. Cooperation will be to your benefit."

16

"Hiya Fern!" Betsy Larimer, the desk sergeant, looked up from her computer. "What mischief have you brought us today?"

Fernwood Grosvenor ignored the teasing.

"Where's Sim?"

"He's back in the interview room with some Indian he brought in."

"Indian?" Fern's brow furrowed as he worked his way through the forest of desks at police headquarters. "What's Sim doing with some Indian when we have important..." he mumbled to himself when he spied Detective Sergeant Holt coming out of the interview room.

"Hi, Sim! What's happening?"

The big sergeant brushed passed him to reach for a cup of coffee on his desk.

"Hiya, Fern. You might be interested in this. I brought in someone who might know something about Mr. Cabot's murder.

Why don't you sit in the mirror room and listen in."

The "mirror room" was the nickname for a room adjacent to the interview room that featured a large observation window allowing occupants to see and hear what was going on during a questioning. On the other side, however, the window appeared to be a big mirror.

Fern let himself in just as Sim reentered the interview room to join a somewhat disheveled looking young man slouched in a chair at the only table in the room.

"Okay, Bear, I'm sorry to interrupt your day," Sim started as he put down his coffee and took a chair opposite the man, who wore a dirty headband and a ratty looking fur vest, "but I need to get some information from you."

The man sat up. "Yeah, Sarge, that's what you always say, but we both know that you're out to stick me with something I didn't do."

Simeon ignored the taunt, clicked on a tape recorder and spoke into it. After declaring the date and time, he spoke into the instrument: "I'm interviewing Matthew Madison of this city, also known as Kicking Bear." Pausing a moment, he turned to Kicking Bear.

"I brought you down here to ask you about your shoes."

Bear looked down at his feet and then back up at the sergeant.

"What about my shoes?"

"Where did you get them?"

"Somebody gave them to me."

"May I see one of them?"

Kicking Bear looked at Sim for a moment, then suddenly

pulled his leg out from under the table and slammed his foot on top. Sim took a sip of his coffee before reaching over to remove the shoe. Despite the staining of winter snow, it was obviously an exquisite sample of the cobbler's trade. Soft, supple leather, intricate tooling and a special, engraved inner lining.

"Are these the initials of your benefactor?" Sim asked, reading the letters J H C in the lining.

"Who knows?" retorted Bear, pulling his foot back down under the table.

"The reason I ask you," said Sim, carefully placing the shoe down in front of him on the table, "is that we have a murdered man in the morgue who was missing his shoes when we found him – and his name happens to fit these initials."

Kicking Bear slumped in his chair. "You're not pinning that on me!"

"Well, Bear, it does seem mighty suspicious that you may be wearing what I'm sure will turn out to be Mr. Cabot's shoes. I think you found him in the park, clocked him and took his shoes."

"No way!" Kicking Bear sat up. "He was just lying there drunk, rich son-of-a-bitch, lying in the park that he and his rich buddies took away from us Native Americans. The shoes were about the only part of him that wasn't lying in the water, so I took 'em."

"But he wasn't drunk, Bear, he was dead."

"Who knew?"

"We're thinking that you knew."

"Wait a minute, Holt, you're not going to stick me with this.

You guys are always picking on us minorities. Something goes wrong and right away you round up some poor Indian or black or Spic and decide they musta done it. Saves time and work. I want a lawyer."

Sim was about to answer when there was a knock at the door, which opened to reveal a beckoning finger. Sim clicked off the recorder, got up and left the room.

Minutes later, he returned, picked up the shoe from the table and grumbled to Kicking Bear.

"Okay, Bear, you can go. Give me the other shoe."

"Oh, I can go?" said Bear, standing up. "To hell with you, Sim. You give me back my shoe!"

"It's not your shoe," said Sim wearily. "I need them for evidence."

"So how am I going to get home? Barefoot?"

"Go down the hall to Lost & Found. Tell 'em I said to give you another pair of shoes. Then get the hell out of here - and stay out of trouble."

Fernwood, behind the glass, could not believe what was going on. He waited until both men had left the interview room and then emerged to confront Sim.

"You let him go??!!" Fern looked up wide-eyed at his policeman pal. "What was that all about? He practically confessed on the spot!"

Sim led the way back to his desk.

"It looks like Kicking Bear didn't murder anybody. Mr. Cabot's death was apparently an accident." Sim plopped down in his swivel chair, put the recorder on his desk and the shoes in a drawer.

"An accident?" Fern swung himself into the chair next to Sim's desk, feet dangling.

Sim exhaled deeply and reached for a cigar.

"One of our guys was back at the scene this morning, slipped and fell and cracked his noggin on a rock at the edge of the pond. The wound was in almost exactly the same place as Cabot's."

"So? What's that got to do with anything?"

"Well," said Simeon, lighting his cigar, "it prompted the coroner to go back and take a look at the wound on Cabot's head."

"Why?"

"Well, you know, the official cause of death was not the blow to the head. It was drowning. It looks like Cabot was dinged, fell over unconscious into the pond and drowned."

"Yeah. So whoever did the dinging was ultimately responsible for his death."

"Unless it was an accident. Turns out there was a lot of alcohol in Cabot's blood. So a case could be made that he was drunk, slipped at the edge of the pond and fell on a rock. The coroner said there was some sort of lichen in the wounds of both men – a kind of plant that he says is rare and endemic to this part of the country – in ponds like ours."

"And?"

Sim took a long draw on his cigar. "So, they checked the rock that both guys probably fell on, and sure enough, there was this lichen all over it. So, now it looks like Cabot wasn't hit. He hit himself."

17

Alexandria and Walter Vanderhoff strolled together along the familiar path. The park was bathed in early morning mist. Solitary walkers, they moved slowly, their steps joined in rhythm. In the peace of early spring, hands clasped, they were content simply to be with one another.

As they approached a bench, Alex turned to the silent man walking quietly beside her. He gave a quick nod. She welcomed the chance to rest for a moment.

"Thank you, Walter," she whispered.

"No problem," he replied. They lingered, grateful for the respite.

As the sun gradually broke through the mist, they rose together. She reached for his hand.

"I need your opinion."

"Go on," he answered.

"What do you think of the idea of a rather small gathering... perhaps a dinner party with some of our new friends?"

"Any special reason?"

"No. Just to let them know we appreciate them."

"Well, it's a nice thought." The Baron stopped for a moment, then looked at Alex. "But I wonder how wise it is."

"Wise?"

"My Dear, you're still recovering from a severe heart attack, and I know how you throw yourself into projects like this. I'm also remembering what a stressful time we had, the last time we had a dinner party – people throwing glasses of water, falling out of their chairs..."

Alex looked away for a moment.

"Yes, that was some circus, wasn't it?" She smiled a small, pained smile. "But this would be different. Just Ruby and her friends. And I'll have a lot of help – the new butler and our favorite chef ... In fact; I bet that even Ruby would support me."

It was obvious that Alex was dead set on the plan. The Baron gave her a quick hug, took her hand and said, "Well, if you're sure..."

"Thank you, Walter," Alex said as she leaned her head for a moment on his shoulder.

They resumed their walk along the path.

"What a beautiful day!" Alex observed.

The Baron agreed. "That it is, My Dear."

The month before, the coroner had released the remains of James Harriman Cabot, and a funeral was arranged by the late lawyer's personal publicist and his law firm. It took place at the city's First Episcopal Church and was attended by municipal dignitaries, political friends and clients of the deceased, plus hundreds of citizens who were simply curious.

Notably absent from the last rites, though, were the Rakovsky sisters.

Instead, some months later, when Alexandria proposed the party idea to Ruby, her sister was delighted, and erasing all memory of their acrid exchange at Alex's last party, volunteered once again to help out.

On the night of the event, Ruby came early, accompanied by Fernwood, and was met at the door by Alexandria's new butler Antoine.

"Ah!" said Antoine, opening the door wide, "Mademoiselle Ruby! Welcome! Your sister is expecting you!"

Ruby handed the butler a bouquet of roses. "These are for my sister and this...." (indicating Fern) ...is my friend Mr. Grosvenor."

Antoine looked down, noticing the small man for the first time, choked off an astonished look and bowed slightly.

"Welcome, Monsieur Grosvenor! Please come in, both of you!" He ushered the pair into the living room where Alex and the Baron were waiting. After quick hugs for both the Vanderhoffs, Ruby introduced her friend Fernwood and then excused herself to see what she could do to help in the kitchen.

Left with their diminutive guest, the Baron and Alex shifted awkwardly and put on small, tentative smiles. Finally, the Baron indicated a chair and invited Fernwood to sit down.

"Thanks," said Fernwood, but first I wanted to give you these." He proffered an elaborate box to the Baron.

"I understand you appreciate good cigars," Fern went on. "These are from Cuba. I have a friend who snuck them in from Mexico."

The Baron's eyes lit up as he took the cigars.

"Hoyo de Monterreys!" he exclaimed. "This IS a treat!" He opened the box, took out a cigar, lifted it to his nose and took a deep sniff. "Ah! Mr. Grosvenor – uh Fernwood – you have brought me a treasure. Come, we must try one immediately before dinner!" and he offered the open box to his guest who had climbed into a chair.

"Oh no!" exclaimed Alex. "If you two are going to light up those smelly cigars, I'm going to have to excuse myself."

But the men were already enjoying their new pleasure, and as Alex left the room, they were beginning to trade stories about cigars, brandies and other sensual pleasures of the world.

"Antoine," Alex called to the butler, "when the other guests come, take them into the parlor. These two gentlemen are well on their way to spoiling the atmosphere in the living room!" As the butler nodded, a puff of blue acrid smoke drifted out of the room into the hallway.

Moments later the doorbell rang, and both Alex and Ruby joined the butler as he opened the door. It was Bernie and Violet. Alex, momentarily distracted by Violet's knee high red boots and her bulging middle, managed to recover what she imagined was her composure and welcomed the pair.

"I'm so glad to meet you!" She paused and then blurted, "I've been told that you're expecting an addition to your family…" She again stared at Violet's belly.

"Oh yes!" said Violet. "Three months to go! We're thinking that we're going to have to find a bigger apartment!"

At that moment, the Baron emerged from the smoky living room to greet the newcomers.

"Walter, these are Ruby's friends Bernie and Violet," said Alex as she handed their wraps to Antoine.

"Ah! Bernie and Violet! I'm so glad to meet friends of Ruby's! Welcome, welcome!" Extending a hand to Bernie, he suddenly paused as he remembered.

"Bernie and Violet. I understand you're the ones who found the toy cat we've heard so much about."

"That's us!" acknowledged Violet. Bernie nodded.

"Actually," Violet went on, "it was Bernie who found it, but we've given it to Clayton Rockford to turn over to the museum, you know, with the money in it and all that..."

The Baron was about to comment when the bell rang again and Antoine opened the door to admit Tyler, Maria, Loretta and Clayton. While Antoine took their wraps, Ruby ushered them into the parlor, left Maria to do the introductions and went across the hall to fetch Fernwood.

"Boy!" Ruby commented as the little man snuffed out his cigar, "you guys really stunk up this room with your smokes! We're going to have to get a fan in here or something to clear it out!"

"Tut tut," said Fernwood as he passed by her on his way to the parlor. "You just don't appreciate the fine aroma of a really superior cigar! That box I brought to the Baron? He just loved them!"

"Well, I wish he'd taken you and the cigars into another room," said Ruby waving the smoke away from her face. "Our guests should really be seated in here where there's more room and more comfy chairs."

As Fernwood greeted all the new arrivals, Antoine announced that supper was now ready.

The table was beautifully set with the roses Ruby had brought as a centerpiece. Alex indicated where each guest was to sit, with couples across from each other and hosts at the ends. All took their places, and the appetizer was served. When all were seated, the Baron stood up, raised his wineglass and welcomed everyone, expressing his and Alex's pleasure for the opportunity to meet Ruby's friends.

Alex looked over at Ruby, smiling, but it was obvious to both Ruby and the Baron that for Alex, it was kind of like opening night in her role as hostess to this new group of guests. Everyone inquired as to how she was feeling and commented on how well she looked, leaving her quite pleased with what seemed to be honest concern from people who had only a short while ago been strangers.

"You know," Ruby said to The Baron and Alex, "all these friends, new and old, came together because of the things that happened there in the park this winter."

"And it was some winter!" agreed Tyler, "what with Cabot's demise and Bernie's discovery of Jackson's memorial to Sunshine."

"Oh yes," said the Baron, "Whatever happened to the cat? Wasn't it stuffed with money or something?"

"Antique money," said Clayton. "Really valuable. We've given it to the Museum of the American Indian."

"Ah yes, now I remember," mused the Baron, looking at Alex. "Part of your father's estate. But refresh me. How did it get into a toy cat, and how did Tyler's son come to possess it?"

Several of the guests started to explain the convoluted tale of the cat and the money, but Alex broke in.

"Long story, Dear. And I'm afraid I complicated it when I thoughtlessly donated all Dad's stuff to the Native American annual flea market. Actually, correct me if I'm in error, Ruby, but I think that both of us never had any interest in Dad's collection, and as avid a collector as he was, he never tried to encourage us." She paused, then added, "I had no idea that Quinn, that butler we had, had stuffed it with Daddy's money."

"Quinn's trial comes up next month, I think," said Fernwood.

"Well, we've recovered over 75% of the collection, including the money," said Clayton, "and it's going to a good home. In fact, I urge you to attend the ceremony when Al's collection will be presented to the museum. Ruby and Alex, I think you'd both enjoy the honor your dad will be given for his gift and his deep interest in the history of Native Americans. If you'd like to go, I'll see that you get tickets."

"Well, it sounds like a good place for the cat's money to end up," said Violet approvingly.

"The cat, the cat," mused Maria. "It certainly has figured in all our lives these last few months. Almost like it's a symbol of something."

Dessert was a scrumptiously delicious dish created by the chef, a dense, almond flower cake with tiny chunks of chocolate all through and topped with a coffee ice cream, flavored further with Kahlua liqueur. Alex received everyone's compliments graciously, and asked Antoine to invite the chef into the dining room to receive a hand of applause.

Loretta, pulling her shawl around her shoulders, picked up on Maria's remark.

"The cat is indeed a symbol. It was viewed by some Native American tribes as a spirit guide. And in fact, the ancient Egyptians believed that cats were miracle animals – that they brought good luck to all who came in contact with them."

"Well, in a way, it brought good luck to us," said Violet. "We didn't keep the money, but it marked the start of what looks like a good life ahead!"

"For me too," said Fernwood, smiling across the table at Ruby, who gave an embarrassed chuckle. Tyler and Maria nodded in silent agreement, and Clayton raised his wineglass to Loretta.

"Ah yes," said the Baron. "Good luck for everyone except Mr. Cabot who was found so close to your cat."

There was a moment of silence, broken by Ruby.

"I happen to know," she said, "that Jim Cabot hated cats."

Acknowledgements

The authors wish to thank all those who gave so unstintingly of their time and talent, helping us to complete this book. They included Peter White, who designed the cover and gave us invaluable help in developing and formatting the book, patient reviewers Heidi Doyle and Howard Shaw, Carolyn White who proofread our manuscript and gave us important advice, Eleanor Howe, who took our pictures, Al Doyle who gave us generous support, and KDP Press, who guided us through the final stages of our creation.

J.S., B.S., W.W.

Made in the USA
Middletown, DE
05 May 2021